# Kiss Me Once,
# Kiss Me Twice

Stephanie couldn't help but smile as Glen came toward her. He was one of her little "mistakes" from the past week. She somehow had ended up in his arms in the heat of the moment. He had been just the thing to make Jonathan's declaration of love go away.

Now Glen took a half-step closer. His breath warmed her face. She lifted her mouth, her eyes closing.

"I think right about here is where we left off," Glen whispered.

His lips pressed against hers, and Stephanie felt herself melting. All at once she had the feeling that someone was watching them. She twisted free and turned around. Before her stood a tall, dark, and handsome man, his hands jammed deep in the pockets of his overcoat. Brown eyes flashed darkly.

Stephanie gasped, "Jonathan!"

# NANCY DREW ON CAMPUS™

Available from ARCHWAY Paperbacks

---

# Nancy Drew
## on campus™ #18

# Keeping Secrets

## Carolyn Keene

**AN ARCHWAY PAPERBACK**
Published by POCKET BOOKS
New York  London  Toronto  Sydney  Tokyo  Singapore

This book is a work of fiction. Names, characters, places and incidents are products of the author's imagination or are used fictitiously. Any resemblance to actual events or locales or persons, living or dead, is entirely coincidental.

AN ARCHWAY PAPERBACK *Original*

An Archway Paperback published by
POCKET BOOKS, a division of Simon & Schuster Inc.
1230 Avenue of the Americas, New York, NY 10020

Copyright © 1997 by Simon & Schuster Inc.
Produced by Mega-Books, Inc.

ISBN: 0-671-56807-8

First Archway Paperback printing February 1997

10  9  8  7  6  5  4  3  2  1

NANCY DREW, AN ARCHWAY PAPERBACK and colophon are registered trademarks of Simon & Schuster Inc.

NANCY DREW ON CAMPUS is a trademark of Simon & Schuster Inc.

Cover photos by Pat Hill Studio

Printed in the U.S.A.

IL 8+

# CHAPTER 1

I t's here!" Nancy Drew heard Kara Verbeck shout over the blaring music and laughter coming from Suite 301. But when Nancy stepped through the doorway, Kara squinted at her in disappointment. "Oh, it's you."

Nancy dropped her backpack and gave Kara a mock-injured look. "It's nice to see you, too, roomie."

"Don't take it personally, Nance," Liz Bader said. "We thought you were the pizzas."

Liz and Kara, both wearing oversize Wilder Women sweatshirts, sat cross-legged on the floor, sharing a huge bag of nacho chips. Their boyfriends, Daniel Frederick and Tim Downing, were slouched down in the couch, their feet propped up on the coffee table. Liz's friend Jenny Osborne straddled a chair while eating out of a jumbo bag of pretzels.

"We got enough pizza for you, Nancy," Kara said. "It's pepperoni."

"You're evil, Kara." Nancy laughed. "You know I can't resist."

The dimples in Daniel's cheeks deepened as he adjusted his tortoise-framed glasses. "We need to fuel up."

"For what?" Jenny asked.

"What do you mean, for what?" Kara grabbed a pretzel from Jenny's bag. "Club Z's grand opening tomorrow night, and the Zeta bash Saturday."

Everyone in the dorm was psyched for the weekend. Club Z, a new dance club in downtown Weston, was officially opening. It was owned by Jason Lehman, a former Wilder student, and it promised to be the hottest place in town.

"This weekend's gonna be great." Nancy's sky blue eyes narrowed with her smile. "Has Jake been here yet?"

"Nope." Liz shrugged.

"I saw him heading toward the newspaper about an hour ago," Daniel said.

"He didn't call?" Nancy asked.

Kara shook her head. "No, but you know he will."

Nancy wasn't so sure. Disappointed, she collapsed on the floor next to Kara. "He should have been here by now," she tried to say casually.

"Speaking of missing persons," Liz spoke up, "where's Eileen? She was supposed to be here

2

with our Club Z invites." She leaned over to Nancy and lowered her voice to a stage whisper, "This pizza's mostly for her, you know. A bribe for our invitations. And there're only so many of them.

"Kara, we live with Eileen. And she's dating Emmet, whose brother owns the club," Nancy said. "We *have* to get in."

Just then there was a knock on the door.

Liz cupped her ear. "Pizza?" she asked, jumping up.

Jake? Nancy wondered optimistically.

Liz whipped open the door, and a tangy pepperoni-and-cheese breeze swept into the suite. Standing in the doorway was a tall guy in a red-and-blue Presto Pizza uniform, cradling two large pies.

Nancy thought of her boyfriend as she watched her friends swarm around the pizza guy. What's going on with Jake? Why isn't he here?

Lately things had been a little tense and confusing with Jake. Nancy didn't even know if he would show up today. The problem seemed to have started weeks ago when Nancy joined the Focus Film Society and became friends with Terry Schneider, the president of the group. Jake hadn't exactly been thrilled about it.

Then Nancy took him home to meet her father and was disappointed when Jake didn't understand why Nancy was upset about Carson Drew's new girlfriend, Avery Fallon.

Nancy felt a pang as she remembered that weekend. Jake didn't even try to understand my point of view, she thought. Avery was there the whole time. In *my* house. Acting as if it was her house. My father doesn't need me anymore. Why can't Jake see that that upsets me?

Nancy sighed. Jake and she were drifting apart; they had to find out why. Nancy didn't want to think about what would happen to their relationship if they couldn't.

Come on, Jake, Nancy silently pleaded. Don't blow me off. Let's go somewhere dark and quiet and romantic. We can work this out.

Pam Miller was just stepping inside the double doors to the African-American Cultural Alliance Center when she noticed a tall, handsome guy on his way out of the building.

"Jesse!" Pam cried, following him back out onto the steps. "Is that you?"

As soon as Jesse Potter turned and saw Pam, his face split into a huge grin. Under his jacket, Pam could see that he was wearing a tight black T-shirt with the words Natural Shades stretched across his muscular chest. He was a representative for Natural Shades Cosmetics, a company that was holding a nationwide contest to find new models to launch a cosmetics line for younger women.

"Pam Miller," Jesse said easily. "I've seen a thousand women since I last saw you, but none of them were beautiful enough to make me forget you. It's a pleasure to see you again."

"Thanks." Pam grinned, blushing a little at Jesse's compliment. "So, what are you doing at Wilder? We heard that your new model won't be introduced until Sunday."

Pam and a number of other Wilder students, including Reva Ross, one of Nancy Drew's suitemates, had entered the Natural Shades contest. Reps from the cosmetics company had been to the campus to search for likely candidates. Since then both Pam and Reva had been waiting anxiously to see who would be chosen as the company's Midwest model. Natural Shades had announced that they'd picked a Wilder student as the Midwest representative.

"The announcement *is* set for Sunday," Jesse explained. "But you don't think we'd let a big event like this happen with only a boring announcement, do you?"

"I think there are quite a few Wilder women who would never use the word *boring* for this announcement," Pam said, chuckling.

"Of course the announcement of the winner will be exciting," Jesse agreed. "But the Sunday afternoon tea is only for the press, university bigshots, and the contestants."

"So what else are you planning?" Pam asked.

"A blowout party, of course." Jesse said. "Here"—he gestured behind him to the Alliance Center—"on Saturday night. The Natural Shades executives will be there, and we're inviting all the Wilder women who entered the contest."

"The night before?" Pam said. "Everyone will be crazy with anticipation."

"Exactly," Jesse replied. "Crazy makes for fun parties. Which gives me only three days to get everything ready. So here I am, back at Wilder, the campus of beautiful women and nervous boyfriends."

Pam winced as she remembered what had happened during her interviews with Jesse. They had turned into a comedy of errors because Pam's boyfriend, Jamal Lewis, showed up every time Jesse was standing anywhere near her. Jamal had accused Jesse of flirting with Pam, and he'd actually interrupted *both* of her interviews!

"Come on," Pam prodded him. "Jamal wasn't that bad—was he?"

Jesse just raised his eyebrows, saying nothing.

Pam put on a pained face. "Well, I'm glad you're back. And, I have to admit, ever since I heard that a Wilder student had won I've been *dying* to know who it is."

Jesse smiled. "You're not asking whether I know anything, are you?"

*"Moi?"* Pam said, aghast. She clutched her chest in mock horror. "Never, although right now—especially after seeing you here—three days suddenly seems like forever!"

"Don't worry," Jesse said. "It'll fly by. Say,

how about meeting me for coffee sometime tomorrow? I'll need a break."

Pam paused. Though they'd been joking about the way Jamal had overreacted during the model search, Pam knew that Jamal really was jealous.

"Come on, Pam," Jesse urged. "I don't have any *other* friends here. It's just friends and just coffee."

"You're right," Pam replied quickly. "I don't know what I was thinking. I'd love to meet you. Tomorrow at Java Joe's at eleven?"

"Great," Jesse said. "I think this could be the beginning of a long friendship."

Pam threw him a quizzical look, but Jesse just waved and headed off. "See you tomorrow."

As she watched Jesse head across campus, she could feel the galloping in her heart. A *long* friendship? Was Jesse hinting that Pam might be the winner?

Pam could hardly wait until her coffee date with Jesse the next day even though she knew Jamal would probably be upset.

Maybe I won't tell him, she mused. If I *am* the winner, that would explain why Jesse wants to get to know me—we'd be working together! What could be the harm having coffee with him?

Lifting her chin and taking a last drag on her cigarette, Stephanie Keats gave herself an approving smile in the window of the Wilder Federal Credit Union in downtown Weston before sauntering across the street.

It was a crisp autumn twilight, the sky an endless pink and blue dome. The quaint downtown was cast in a romantic fiery glow. Stephanie knew she'd risen to the occasion: She'd pulled her silky, long dark hair up, off her face, and the pants she wore were pleated and stylishly baggy. Even her makeup was subdued, letting her naturally stunning features—chestnut eyes, high cheekbones, full lips—speak for themselves.

A self-satisfied smile came to her mouth. The whole effect of her appearance was, she knew, adult and classy. Exactly the look that Jonathan Baur, her new boyfriend, appreciated.

"Five of five," Stephanie murmured, reading the old-fashioned clock suspended above Berrigan's Department Store, where Jonathan was a floor manager and Stephanie had a part-time job as a salesclerk. He'd be out in five minutes.

Waiting for the traffic to pass, she dropped her cigarette and ground it into the curb with the heel of her pump. Her heart skipped a beat. "I love you, too," she murmured, wanting to hear how it sounded again. It sounded—well, strange.

The truth was, she'd never spoken those words—and meant them—to *anyone*, until a couple of weeks ago. After a long string of one-date flings, she had fallen hard for Jonathan. When he told her he loved her, Stephanie, who hadn't thought she had it in her, had to admit to herself a few days later that she loved him, too. It took her another few to say it though. And even now she wouldn't put money on her love.

The problem, she thought as she walked toward the store, was that love meant being with only one person. Unfortunately, being with only one man had never been a possibility for Stephanie.

She winced as she remembered the handful of guys she'd fooled around with in the days between Jonathan's heartfelt confession and her own words of love. Guys whose names she could barely remember.

"Why did I do it?" she asked herself as the clock struck five.

But she knew why.

Jonathan made her feel something new, something scary, and that made her nervous. He knew what he wanted in life—his own retail store . . . and Stephanie.

Loving Jonathan sounded like a great idea. The only problem was that Stephanie had never been able to, or even wanted to, stay committed to anyone. Ever.

"Well, you look absolutely wonderful," a deep masculine voice said. "Remember me?"

Stephanie turned and swallowed hard at the sight of the tall, blond soccer player in front of her.

"Do I ever," she said. The name came to her in an instant. "Glen."

Glen snapped his fingers, his voice dropping to the singsong of a game-show host. "Yes! And for your correct response, you have just won a *bonus* date with"—he clutched his heart—"yours truly!"

Stephanie couldn't help but smile. Glen was one of her little "mistakes" from the past week. She somehow had ended up in his arms, and in the heat of the moment, he'd whispered something about being unattached, and not looking for the love of his life. He had been just the thing to make Jonathan's declaration of love go away.

They'd started kissing, and—well, things progressed from there to some heavy-duty necking behind the refreshment stand at the football game.

"I don't mean to sound like a bad movie," Glen said, throwing an arrogant, sidelong glance at Berrigan's, "but what's a gorgeous girl like you doing hanging out on street corners?"

Stephanie could feel the attraction building between them. It was like heat. "It *is* a little chilly out here," she said with a wry grin.

"I know a great way to get you warmed up," Glen said.

Stephanie could smell a come-on line a mile away. But she didn't care. This was fun. This was the old life, the old Stephanie Keats. Thoughts of Jonathan started drifting away like wisps of smoke on the soft breeze.

She looked into Glen's eyes. "Oh? And what would that be?"

Glen took a half-step closer. His breath warmed her face. She lifted her mouth, her eyes closing.

"I think right about here is where we left things off," Glen whispered.

His lips pressed against hers, and Stephanie felt herself melting. All at once she had the feeling that someone was watching them. She twisted free and turned around. Before her stood a tall, dark, and handsome man, his hands jammed deep in the pockets of his overcoat. Brown eyes flashed darkly.

Stephanie gasped, "Jonathan!"

"I know I'm late." Jake winced, holding his hands up as Nancy stood beside the door to the suite.

Boyishly handsome in his usual denim and cowboy boots, he took in the room—pizza boxes and pretzel and chip bags littered the floor. "What did I miss?"

"Preparty party," Nancy replied, her face breaking into a smile. "Don't worry. I saved you a couple of slices."

"I was just going to fix up the lead on an article," he started to explain, "and, well, you know me—"

Nancy said, "You're only an hour late. But you made it in time for the five-thirty news."

Jake clutched Nancy's hands. "Forget about the news. I'd rather look at you. You're beautiful."

Jake was pleased to see Nancy's face light up at his words.

"I was up all last night, and I'm sure I look it. But I love the compliment. Eat." Nancy walked over to the coffee table and slid two slices of pizza on a paper plate and held them out to him.

Jake walked all the way into the lounge and waved at the others gathered there. "Hi, guys."

"The mystery man," Liz teased. "I voted to eat your pizza, but Nancy threatened our lives."

"And now for the news," the anchorman announced.

Jake sat next to Nancy on the couch, the plate of pizza slices almost forgotten on the coffee table, and lifted his hands behind his head. Nancy rested her head in the crook of his neck.

"I can't believe Gail is going to be on TV," he said.

Gail Gardeski was the editor-in-chief of the *Wilder Times,* the campus newspaper, where Nancy and Jake were both reporters.

"You guys have to fill me in on this case," Liz said.

"It's really creepy because a convicted sex offender is back on the streets," Nancy said.

"*Alleged* sex offender," Jake corrected her. "And that's the problem. Three years ago a guy named Cal Evanson was convicted of sexually

12

molesting and robbing three women in Weston—"

"It terrified all the women in town and on campus," Nancy interrupted.

"Wonderful," Liz quipped.

"Evanson always insisted he was innocent," Jake continued. "He said that he had been convicted because his lawyer was too inexperienced. So last year, from jail, he hired a new lawyer. This new guy discovered that one of the cops in the investigation might have planted a piece of key evidence and possibly coerced one of the victims into identifying Cal Evanson as her attacker."

"It was enough for reasonable doubt, and the judge tossed out the guilty verdict three weeks ago," Nancy said. "Evanson is out on bail while he waits for a new trial."

"So he's actually *out* of prison," Liz said, tightening her grip on her knees. "This is creepy! I'm not going *anywhere* alone at night."

"Shh, Gail's interview is on," Jake said.

Gail was seated in the news studio across from a reporter. She was small and bone-thin, and looked professional and composed behind her wire-rimmed glasses.

"Ms. Gardeski," the interviewer began, "local journalists, as well as citizens of Weston and Wilder University students, are all hotly debating the guilt of Cal Evanson."

"And the *Wilder Times,* our campus newspaper, is working on related articles," Gail replied.

Jake caught Nancy glancing at him and locked her in a smile. She slipped an arm behind his back and squeezed his middle. No matter what was going on between them, Jake knew, they shared a passion for their newspaper work and for each other.

Putting an arm around her, he pulled her closer. Smiling, she collapsed against him.

"And you, or one of your reporters," the TV interviewer continued, "have taken new statements from a victim of these assaults, Liana Schmidt—"

"Liana Schmidt, that's right," Gail replied.

"But the big news is that you are publishing an article in tomorrow's *Wilder Times* that mentions information from a previously unknown source that confirms the DA's belief that Evanson is really guilty of the attacks."

Jake and Nancy sat bolt upright.

"Did you know about this?" Nancy asked.

Astounded, Jake shook his head. "That must be what Gail's been working on so hard."

"What we want to know," the TV interviewer continued, "and what the DA is sure to want to know himself, is who this unknown source is, what proof he or she has, and why he or she hasn't come forward before."

Gail merely shook her head. "I'm afraid that's privileged information. My source came forward on the condition that his or her identify remain a secret. And as a reporter yourself," Gail continued, "you know that a reporter's first obligation, after writing the truth, is to protect her sources."

"Wow," Liz said. "She's tough."

"And right," Nancy added.

"And in trouble," Jake murmured worriedly. "The DA's going to be all over her."

"Okay," Liz said. "I'm thoroughly spooked that this Cal guy is out on the streets. I'm sleeping with the lights on till this is over."

"Evanson must be under some kind of police surveillance," Jake assured her. "Besides, no one's sure he's the right guy."

Laughing ruefully, Nancy stared at him unblinking. "You really know how to make a girl feel safe."

# CHAPTER 2

What am I going to do, Eileen O'Connor thought as she climbed the steps to the porch of Kappa house. She rubbed the temples of her pounding head. Tomorrow night was the grand opening of Club Z. Everyone Eileen knew wanted to be there. Her suitemates, the girls in her sorority, and even people she barely knew, all wanted her to get them into what was sure to be the coolest party of the year.

Eileen plopped down on the top step of the old Victorian house. Sighing, she said out loud, "This is probably the *only* negative thing about dating Emmet Lehman."

Thinking about Emmet made her smile. He was handsome, athletic, the star of the football team, *and* her boyfriend. She'd never imagined she could be so happy.

Except for her one big problem.

Eileen had thought she could get invitations for all her suitemates and sorority sisters—until an hour ago.

Eileen remembered the expression on Jason Lehman's face when she and Emmet had stopped by the club to say hello. He looked as if he'd been tearing his hair out.

"You can't believe how insane this is," he'd practically screamed, from behind the bar. "The phone won't stop ringing. Everyone wants invitations to the opening. Someone even stuck a note under the windshield wiper of my car."

"So," Eileen said lightly, "having trouble keeping the numbers down?"

"The trouble is keeping the numbers *out!*" Jason had cried, sliding the guest list notebook with five pages of names over to them. "This is too long," Jason had said. "Oh, and I'm sorry, guys, I know I told you that you could invite your friends, but forget it. I can't get closed down by the police on my first night of business."

"But we can still come, right?" Emmet had asked.

"Yeah, but just you two" was Jason's reply.

Sighing again, Eileen pushed herself up and headed for the front door. She felt bad for her friends, but she was still excited for herself. This was definitely one of the perks of dating Emmet. The Club Z bash was going to be great!

No sense worrying about it anymore, Eileen

thought as she stepped into the Kappa living room.

"Hey, it's our ticket to Club Z!" someone cried out.

Eileen grimaced. That sounded like a reason to start to worry again.

"Hi, guys." Eileen smiled weakly. She surveyed the couch where Soozie Beckerman, the Kappa secretary, was sitting with two other upperclass Kappa sisters.

"So, Eileen," Soozie asked, tossing her head of blond hair, "when do we get our invitations?"

"It isn't exactly my party," Eileen began.

"I hope you're not thinking it will be funny to keep us waiting until the last minute," Soozie snapped. "You are just a freshman, *and* a freshman pledge."

"I'm not playing games with you if that's what you mean," Eileen replied quickly.

"Then I assume we'll be getting our tickets tomorrow," Soozie said. "After all, what is a great boyfriend for?"

"Well . . ." Eileen began, just as Holly Thornton, Bess Marvin, and Casey Fontaine burst into the living room.

"Hey, you guys, listen to this! According to *Holly*," Casey said, "a great boyfriend is someone with fast typing fingers!"

Eileen shot a relieved smile at her redheaded suitemate and sorority sister.

"What is she talking about?" Soozie asked, staring at Holly curiously.

Holly rolled her eyes. "She's just trying to tease me about going on-line."

"Holly's perfecting the art of information-highway flirting," Bess added.

"Flirting?" Eileen asked, grateful that the subject of the Club Z party had been changed. "With whom?"

"With the entire Internet, it sounds like," Casey said, grinning wickedly.

"Oh, come on!" Holly laughed. "I've just been checking out some of the Usenet newsgroups, that's all. Lots of students are on-line now. It's a great way to meet people who have similar interests."

"And now Holly's *met* someone," Casey crowed. "Although at this moment he's still just a screen name and a few lines on her computer screen."

Holly interrupted, "He's a guy I started talking to who sounds really sweet. I met him in an arts newsgroup."

"I'm sorry," Soozie blurted out. "But that's ridiculous!" She wrinkled her nose in disgust. "How can you 'date' someone you've never even seen?"

"We're not exactly dating," Holly replied.

"And besides," Casey added, "looks aren't everything, Soozie, remember? There *is* such a thing as personality." Casey paused. "Only you

19

need to trust that the personality you're speaking to over the computer is the real one."

"Maybe some people aren't honest," Holly admitted. "But it's just like giving the benefit of the doubt to anyone you meet in person," she added, glancing back at Soozie.

"I don't know." Bess shrugged. "It almost sounds nice."

"It sounds pretty lame to me," Soozie concluded. "But I guess *some* people have to resort to that kind of stuff to get a date. Like putting a personal ad in the paper."

Eileen bit her tongue. Soozie was being her usual obnoxious, ice-princess self.

Speaking up would draw attention to herself, and although she had her own mixed feelings about on-line dating, right now Eileen couldn't have been happier about Holly's mystery guy. At least it kept the conversation off Club Z—for now!

"Just go away, Stephanie," Jonathan insisted, his voice flat and cold. "Leave me alone."

Instead Stephanie stepped in front of him, blocking his path. She had him by the arm and was trying to pull him back into Berrigan's.

If there was one thing Stephanie hated, it was a public scene. But her heart was racing. She was in a panic. She was losing Jonathan. Or should that be "throwing him away"?

Why is it that you never know how much you

want something or someone until it's gone? she wondered.

Jonathan finally stopped struggling. Stephanie had him pressed up against a wall. They were both panting.

"Look, Steph," he pleaded, lifting his arms. "I'm tired of the games. I'm not eighteen anymore or a college freshman. I'm twenty-three and not just out for a good time. I want a real relationship. Obviously you're not ready."

"I *am,*" Stephanie insisted. "Look, you misunderstood what happened back there."

She glanced back over her shoulder at the sidewalk. Thankfully, Glen was gone.

"I misunderstood? What do you think I am, blind? Stupid? Or both?" Jonathan grabbed both of her hands and peered into her eyes. "Look, I'm a patient guy, and I love you, Stephanie. I can't watch you all the time. I don't want to *have* to watch you. I won't live like that. It's trust—or it's nothing."

He stepped around her and started to walk away.

Stephanie swallowed. For the second time in a week she was experiencing a brand-new feeling. Last week it had been love, today it was panic at losing a man. She couldn't let Jonathan slip away. She was desperate. If she told the truth, he was gone.

Just one more lie, she promised. Just this one last time.

"I hardly know that guy," she called after him. *"Really."*

Jonathan stopped and looked around uneasily.

Head down, Stephanie walked up to him. "He's in one of my classes." She gently took his hand and looked straight into his eyes. "I was coming to meet you and I just ran into him. He started coming on to me and tried to kiss me before I could stay no. I was just trying to push him away when you came out of the store."

Jonathan gazed at her in silence, and Stephanie knew he was deciding whether or not to believe her. She was afraid, not just because Jonathan might know she was lying to him, but because of how easy her lie had been.

Concentrate, she instructed herself. Whatever you do, be honest. . . .

"You were holding hands," Jonathan finally said, his eyes narrowing with doubt.

But Stephanie could hear his anger weakening. "I was pushing him away," she lied again. "It just *looked* like we were holding hands."

She rose up on her toes and kissed Jonathan's neck. And when he didn't pull away, she kissed his chin and then his cheek and his lips. She could feel him softening. She could feel his mouth softening.

"What did you tell me last week?" she asked.

"That I love you," Jonathan replied matter-of-factly.

"And what did I tell you?"

"That you love me," Jonathan said softly.

Stephanie's forehead came to rest against his chest. She grabbed on to the lapels of his coat and tugged hard. "And I meant it," she insisted. She could see her reflection in his eyes as he saw her. She knew he understood she wasn't lying this time. She also knew that if he caught her with anyone else, he wouldn't forgive her. He'd be gone. But she knew that when she said she loved him, she meant it from the bottom of her heart.

Jonathan's arms surrounded Stephanie. His chin rested on the top of her head.

She shut her eyes to hold in the truth and whispered again, more to convince herself than him, "And I meant it."

"So, what do you think? Is there hope for me and my sexy reporter, or what?" Nancy asked, watching George Fayne polish off a large plate of meat loaf and potatoes. "George, I can't believe you just ate all that."

"I was hungry," George explained. "I always am after a good run."

One of Nancy's closest friends, George was tall, athletic, and beautiful, with loose brown curls that fell around her face and a pair of luminous brown eyes. Fresh from a run around the lake in tights and a long-sleeve T-shirt, George sat across from Nancy in the cafeteria of Jamison Hall. Nancy needed to talk over what was happening with her and Jake and had stopped by George's dorm to see her.

Her right cheek bulging with her dessert, George waved her fork. "Well"—she paused to swallow—"I think that you and Jake are just going through a tough time. You'll be fine."

Nancy smiled. "I'll choose to believe that because I'm crazy about him."

"Trust me, you guys were made for each other," George assured her. "Now, I want to hear about this interview you're about to do."

Nancy looked at her watch and started to get up. "Oh my gosh, it's in ten minutes!"

George aimed a forkful of devil's food cake at her friend and commanded her to sit. "Come on. Give me the thirty-second version."

Nancy sighed. "Okay. Gail wanted me to cover the human interest side of the Cal Evanson story. Which is, basically, that Cal has a younger sister who's a senior here at Wilder."

George whistled. "Really! How does she feel having a criminal for an older brother?"

"*Alleged* criminal," Nancy corrected her.

"Whatever," George replied. "Sounds like he did it to me."

"Me, too, but everyone's innocent until proven guilty—even the *second* time he's proven guilty," Nancy said, standing up. She waved goodbye as she headed out the door.

Five minutes later Nancy was sitting in the Student Union, across from a soft-spoken girl with wispy straw blond hair that hung to her waist. Nancy had her reporter's notebook in her lap and her eye on the girl's hands. Cal Evanson's sister was wringing her fingers. Her nails had been badly bitten. This is really tearing her apart, Nancy thought.

"Are you sure I can't get you a cup of coffee, Trisha?" Nancy asked her.

Trisha smiled and shook her head. "I'll never get to sleep," she said in a voice barely above a whisper. Suddenly her eyes clouded over, and her face darkened. "Not that I sleep much anyway."

Nancy nodded sympathetically. "I'm sure everything that's happened with Cal has been very hard on you."

"My freshman year, when all the sexual attacks and robberies were going on, the girls on campus were terrified. No one walked alone anywhere. And when they arrested Cal, I lost every single one of my friends."

"It's taken a lot of courage for you to stay," Nancy said.

Nancy readied her pen for Trisha's response.

Sighing, Trisha leaned back deep in her chair. "I believe that if I left Wilder, I would have been giving in."

"To what?" Nancy prodded softly.

"To what everyone was thinking. That Cal was a sexual molester and a thief. It would have been like saying it was true."

"So you think Cal is innocent."

Trisha leveled a steady gaze at Nancy that was so poised, so filled with certainty, that Nancy had to look away. "I don't think so, Nancy. I *know* Cal is innocent. And other people do, too, although they're too afraid to admit it in public. But when it comes to defending Cal, I'm not afraid of anything."

Nancy was struggling to keep up in her notebook with Trisha's flow of words. Trisha was so sympathetic. After all, no matter what the truth was, it wasn't Trisha's fault. And that was Nancy's assignment: not Cal's story, but Trisha's.

"How could you be so sure Cal is innocent," Nancy inquired, "when there's so much evidence against him?"

Trisha sighed. "I know him and he couldn't have done the stuff he is accused of. Look, Cal first became a suspect because he'd dated one of the victims, and he fit the general physical description of the attacker. When the police searched his apartment, they 'conveniently' found a piece of jewelry taken from one of the other victims."

"And that's not good evidence?" Nancy interrupted, not looking up from her notes as she wrote.

"The police planted that jewelry," Trisha said simply. "My brother has always insisted that. And now the third victim is saying she was coerced into testifying against him. The cops and the district attorney made her believe it had to have been Cal who attacked her. She was scared and wanted someone to pay for what happened. But now she's starting to feel bad about it because she was never really sure."

Deep in thought, Nancy nibbled at the nub of her pencil eraser. If what Trisha was saying were true, this story was much more complicated than anyone thought. Especially since Gail now thought she had evidence proving Cal *was* guilty.

"But why," Nancy asked, starting to write again, "would the police lie and plant evidence like that?"

Trisha let out a little laugh. "Imagine what this place was like. There was enormous pressure from the mayor and the citizens of Weston. The police wanted to say they had a suspect. Imagine how happy they were when they found someone to blame."

Nancy narrowed her eyes. "So even if the police only thought Cal *might* have been guilty, they'd go for a conviction, no matter what."

Trisha nodded. "Basically, they were able to convict Cal because he didn't have any witnesses to back up his alibi—"

"That he was home in bed, alone," Nancy added, writing more notes in her pad.

Trisha's eyes welled up with tears of frustration. "Nancy, if you didn't have a roommate, could you prove to me, right now, beyond a shadow of a doubt, that you slept in your room last night?"

Nancy shook her head. "I see your point. But here's my problem, Trisha. And I guess this is everybody's problem. When Cal was arrested, the attacks stopped. How can you explain that?"

Trisha's tears began to fall. "I can't," she whispered. "But I don't have to. Maybe the real attacker thought it was a good time to stop and get away with everything he'd done till then." She pointed at herself. "All *I* know is that Cal is innocent. His first lawyer was terrible, his defense was nonexistent. He didn't even know how to cross-examine. This new lawyer will *definitely* prove Cal is innocent."

Both girls sat back, exhausted and emotionally spent. Nancy scanned her notebook. She'd filled five pages with writing, all of it powerful.

Trisha moved to the edge of her chair. "Can't you print the truth about Cal?" she implored. "And write what a sham his first trial was?"

Nancy shifted uncomfortably in her seat. She was caught between her obligation as a reporter and her sympathy for Trisha. The two didn't seem to be in agreement. "I don't have all the details," she said flatly, "and as much as I'd like to believe you, you *are* Cal's sister."

Trisha held up a hand. "I wouldn't take my word for it, either," she said. "But I do have a copy of the trial transcripts in my apartment, and some notes from Cal's new lawyer. Read them and then decide for yourself if you think he's guilty."

The potential power of this story was over-whelming. Nancy could feel her pulse quicken.

Gail won't like this one bit, Nancy mused. Especially since she's working on the opposite angle. Maybe Gail doesn't have to know. "I'm intrigued," she told Trisha.

Rising to her feet, Trisha seemed filled with new hope.

"But no promises," Nancy warned her.

Trisha nodded. "I understand. No promises."

# CHAPTER 3

"Forget it!" Bess complained, throwing her script on the stage floor. She stomped to the edge of the small stage in the rehearsal theater in Hewlitt Performing Arts Center and glared out into the darkness. She spotted Brian Daglian's head of blond hair in the first row. Next to him sat Casey Fontaine.

"I'm horrible, aren't I?" Bess asked.

Casey shook her head. "Come on, Bess," she said. "You were doing fine."

"Although it *was* a little different from what we talked about last time," Brian admitted.

"I wanted to try something new for the scene," Bess replied, bending down to snatch up her script. "You really think it's that bad?"

"Well," Brian said, hopping onto the stage, "I personally think you're so talented you could audition for Jeanne Glasseburg's class by reading from the phone book."

Jeanne Glasseburg was a famous New York City acting coach. The next semester she would be teaching a special, invitation-only acting class in the theater department, and Bess wanted to be in it.

"Easy for you to say," Bess muttered. "Neither of you has to worry about auditioning. You're both in already."

"Yeah, sure," Brian replied, turning to Casey and shrugging. "We're in because we auditioned by performing in the one-act plays. Which is exactly the same thing you have to do—audition," he finished, staring at Bess.

"I know," Bess said. "But in the one-acts you were with other actors—and each other. I have to do this alone—"

Bess flung out her arms, and Brian ducked to avoid being hit by her cast.

"You're not alone," Brian joked. "You still have that lump of plaster to keep you company. And aren't our supportive faces right there with you?" He pointed to a place on her cast.

Bess chuckled and looked down at the two bizarre smiley faces with Brian and Casey written under them.

"Besides, Bess, you already know Jeanne likes your work," Casey interrupted, coming to lean on the edge of the stage. "At least she's giving you another chance to audition. She hasn't done that for anyone else."

"No one else's boyfriend died in a motorcycle crash, either," Bess muttered. She looked up to see the stricken expressions on her friends' faces.

"Sorry," Bess whispered. "That wasn't fair."

But she couldn't help it. That was the reason she'd missed her own chance to perform in the one-act plays. Her last time with Paul had been a few days before opening night, when the two had gone for a drive in the country on Will Blackfeather's motorcycle. Their bike had been broadsided by a car, and Paul had died in the crash.

Bess shook her head, trying to stave off a wave of sadness.

"Bess?" Brian put his hand on her shoulder.

"You okay?" Casey added softly.

"I'm not sure," Bess said, squeezing her eyes closed for a second. "It gets better, you know," she admitted softly. "Easier not to think about it all the time. Easier to remember that there are still good things in my life. But sometimes that makes me feel guilty."

"But you know Paul wouldn't have wanted your life to be over, too," Casey said softly.

"I know," Bess agreed. "That's what my counselor says, too."

Bess had been skeptical at first about talking to someone, but it was actually helping—as much as anything could.

"I still think about Paul a lot," Bess said to her friends. A sweet smile passed across her face as an image came to her: Paul's golden hair and the tiny laugh lines framing his soft brown eyes. "But it's not fair to use Paul as an excuse for blowing the audition," Bess admitted. "I'm just afraid because I'm finally beginning to care about something again."

"You *should* care about acting," Casey said. "You're really good at it."

"But what if now, with a second chance and everything, I'm not good enough?" Bess wondered aloud.

"Don't worry," Casey said. "We're helping you. Aren't we?"

Brian snatched Bess's script from her. "You've got some terrific moments in this monologue."

"Okay, okay." Bess chuckled. "I'd better start working on my 'internal self' then."

"And try staying away from self-criticism," Casey suggested.

"I'd say that we're through with this rehearsal for the night," Brian said, checking his watch. "It's time for dinner. Let's eat!"

Brian tossed the script back to Bess and she shoved it into her bag. The three of them gathered up the rest of their stuff and left the small theater through the side exit. Just as they reached the lobby of the performing arts center, the front doors opened and Jeanne Glasseburg entered.

Immediately Bess's heart started pounding.

"Bess"—Ms. Glasseburg smiled—"it's good to see you back on campus."

"Thanks," Bess managed to say.

Ms. Glasseburg nodded, but made no move to leave.

"I'm feeling a lot better," Bess stumbled, frantically looking at her friends. "Being back, I mean. I mean, feeling as well as I could expect . . ."

Bess's voice trailed off. Casey nudged her in the ribs.

"Thanks again for letting me audition for you," Bess blurted out.

"Well," Ms. Glasseburg said finally, "I'd say you're welcome, only you haven't done it yet."

"Right." Bess chuckled nervously. And I don't want to! she screamed silently to herself. Yes, I do! a second voice quietly yelled back.

"I'm going back to New York on Monday," Ms. Glasseburg added.

"Really?" Bess asked. "Monday? That's only a few days away."

"That's right," Ms. Glasseburg agreed.

Finally Casey sighed out loud. "Don't you think you should make an appointment, then, Bess?"

"To audition?" Brian added.

"Right." Bess grinned unevenly.

"Only if you're still interested," Ms. Glasseburg said. "I was under the impression that you wanted to be in my class very much, but I'll understand if you don't feel—"

"But I do!" Bess cried without thinking.

"So how about Sunday morning at eleven?" Ms. Glasseburg asked, checking a small scheduling book she'd pulled out of her purse.

"You bet," Bess replied.

"I'll see you then, Bess." Ms. Glasseburg smiled. "Good luck." She turned and made her way to the elevator at the far end of the lobby.

Casey and Brian waited until the three of them were outside, and then they both started in on Bess excitedly.

"Don't worry," Brian said. "It's only a few days, but you'll be great."

"You've got a knockout monologue," Casey continued.

"Better to get it over with," Brian said. "Then it won't be bothering you anymore."

Right, Bess thought, get it over with. Sunday at eleven. But that was only three days from now—would she be ready or would she blow it?

Ray Johansson finished scribbling notes on a very worn piece of notebook paper and then turned to the other members of his new band, Radical Moves.

"Let's try speeding up the drum transition here," he said, showing Cory McDermott his notes. "And then switch the two bass lines." He passed the paper to Austin Rusche. "Want to run through this part one time to see how it sounds?"

Cory nodded and did a soft-volume run-through of the new transition, the bass drum pounding like an automatic rifle, and then nodded.

"One, two, three," Ray said, tapping his foot to the rhythm.

"You said, I never did anything for you.
You said this wasn't real, but it was real.
You don't remember all the times I held you.
So tell me, is that the way you really feel.
You just can't tell me this wasn't real."

As they finished, Ray stood with his guitar against his hip, a thoughtful expression on his face.

"Works much better," Cory said, tapping the snare drum for emphasis.

"Well," Ray said, resting his guitar on its stand. "That part's better, but . . ."

"What's wrong?" Austin asked. "We've hardly been together a week and we already have four new tunes. I think Radical Moves is rockin'!"

Ray smiled. For the most part, he completely agreed. Being kicked out of the Beat Poets by a record company that wanted a different sound had been the worst experience of his life. But since then he'd formed Radical Moves with Cory and Austin and had been feeling more optimistic about music every day. But Radical Moves still needed something else.

"There's nothing wrong with us," Ray said. "It's just that something's missing."

"You think it's our sound?" Cory asked.

"No," Ray answered. "I think that's great."

"Me, too." Cory nodded. "We really feed off one another."

"But I still feel like something's missing," Ray continued. "It's like we're so close but—"

"Maybe we should really be a four-person band?" Austin finished, nodding slowly.

"Yeah," Ray agreed.

"So what do you have in mind?" Cory asked, twirling his drumsticks.

Ray shrugged. "Maybe we're missing another instrument. But what?"

"Electric piano?" Austin asked.

"I hate electric piano," Cory complained. "Everything with electric piano sounds like it was recorded in the seventies."

"Something more offbeat?" Austin suggested.

"Maybe," Ray agreed uncertainly. "But what? Flute and we sound like Jethro Tull, harmonica and we're Blues Traveler."

"Mandolin and we're either Rod Stewart or the Cowboy Junkies," Austin added.

"How about just giving me another drum set?" Cory joked.

"We want to play music, not just make noise," Austin muttered.

"I think we should hold an open call for musicians. We can put up a notice in Hewlitt," Ray suggested. "And just see what floats in."

"You mean when we hear the right musician and instrument we'll know what it is?" Cory asked skeptically.

"Yeah, maybe. Or maybe we'll just get lucky." Ray shrugged.

"If we were lucky," Cory said, smiling wickedly, "Madonna would be looking for a new back-up band."

Early the next morning, armed with two coffees and doughnuts, Jake pushed open the door to the *Wilder Times* office with his hip and walked inside. The desks were empty, the phones silent. Outside, the campus was just starting to stir, morning classes still an hour away.

But he heard movement coming from the direction of Nancy's cubicle.

He walked toward her desk, peeked over the top of the partition, and smiled at Nancy skimming through a foot-high stack of papers. She was concentrating so hard she hadn't heard him come in. He studied the soft linen sweater she was wearing. They'd bought it together early on in their relationship at a boutique downtown. It reminded him of those first days when they couldn't keep their hands off each other. Standing there, Jake felt a wave of emotion. She was so beautiful in the early morning.

Quietly he tiptoed around the partition. She had her long hair held up high in a ponytail, leaving the back of her neck an easy target. He leaned in and planted a soft kiss there. "I'm glad it's you who's here this early."

"Hey!" she cried, and reeled around.

Jake skipped back, lifting the containers of coffee out of danger. "A little jumpy, aren't we?"

Nancy attempted to frown, but her glittering blue eyes gave away her delight at seeing him. "You sneaked up on me!"

"It's the price you pay for being so amazingly disciplined and getting down here at the crack of dawn," he said with a laugh.

Nancy rolled her eyes. "I couldn't sleep."

Jake put down a coffee and doughnut for her.

"Fuel!" she said gleefully. She peered up at him. "But how'd you know I'd be here?"

"You had an interview last night," he explained, "and I knew you'd want to start writing the story right away."

Nancy eyed him, tentatively at first, then lovingly. "You know me better than anybody, Jake Collins," she declared.

Nodding, Jake fingered Nancy's fine, silky hair, flashing gold and red in the sunlight. "You're so beautiful," he said.

Nancy raised her head. "We're a good team, aren't we?"

Jake smiled. "The best."

Nancy blew a stray hair out of her face and

slapped her thighs, as if to get her own attention. "Okay, then take a look through this stuff and tell me what you think."

Jake took one look at all the material and laughed. "Maybe you can give me a quick summary."

"Okay. Well, I've been skimming the notes of Cal Evanson's original lawyer and his new one, and the trial transcripts and interviews, and none of it adds up. Apparently, Cal knew the first victim, someone named Liana Schmidt, from the Purity Coffee Shop, where she waitressed. They'd dated once or twice, and on the night of her assault they had had a drink together at her apartment. Later that evening, after Cal left, she was attacked and robbed by someone who came in through an unlocked window. She insists it was Cal wearing a ski mask."

"Same height and build," Jake cut in.

"Right," Nancy continued. "The other two victims were also waitresses at local restaurants and were attacked by a man wearing a ski mask. All three had jewelry and money stolen. And all three testified that Cal Evanson was their attacker. But the *only* physical evidence linking Cal to any of the crimes was a single ring, supposedly stolen from the third victim, that was found in Cal's apartment. The rest of the missing jewelry was never recovered."

Jake was nodding, listening closely. "So what doesn't add up?"

Nancy handed him a few papers. "These notes from Cal's new lawyer show that he's found an informant in the police department who swears the ring was planted by one of the officers in the case. And this same cop talked the third victim into identifying Cal as her attacker. The cop who did this died last year, so the informant felt safe to come forward."

Nancy lifted another piece of paper, waved it in the air, then continued. "Then the new lawyer reinterviewed the third victim, who finally admitted she wasn't positive Cal was her attacker. And she said she can't be certain that the ring found in Evanson's apartment disappeared the night of her attack. Plus the hair sample from the ski mask doesn't match Cal's."

"Good reasons for a new trial," Jake said, nodding. "Which should be interesting if Gail's new source comes through."

Nancy took a bite of her doughnut. "Last night," she said, "Cal Evanson's sister made a good case about the motives of the police."

Nancy quickly explained Trisha's side of things. "She was pretty convincing," she said when she finished.

It's still going to be hard to find Evanson innocent unless another suspect emerges, Jake thought.

He took Nancy's hand and gave it a squeeze. She lifted her eyes to his, the glimmer of a smile playing at the corners of her mouth. Jake bent forward, and he could breathe the familiar, sweet fragrance of her hair. Nancy's lips parted, and they were about to kiss, when the phone on her desk shattered the mood.

Nancy snatched up the phone. "Hello!" she said, irritated. "Oh, hi." Quickly, she scribbled on a piece of paper for Jake to see: "It's Steve Shapiro."

Professor Shapiro was the newspaper's faculty advisor.

"What? You're kidding! . . . Sure, I'll have Gail call you the second I see her." Nancy hung up the phone.

"What is it?" Jake asked.

Nancy crossed her arms and whistled. "The DA's office just phoned Steve. After the TV interview last night, the DA called Gail to find out the name of her source. Gail, of course, wouldn't give it to him, and now the DA is threatening to subpoena Gail to surrender it in court."

Jake shook his head, stunned.

"If she still refuses to reveal the name, she could be thrown in jail for contempt!"

# CHAPTER 4

*Dear Blondie: I don't want to scare you off, but when are we going to meet in person? Flash.*

It was Friday morning, and Holly sat in front of her computer in her sorority house room. She was reading the message on her screen from Flash, the guy she'd been talking to on-line for a while now. She really liked him—at least she liked what she knew about him through their conversations on the computer. But was she ready to actually meet him in person?

It was fun, and also liberating, to get to know someone through E-mail. Holly never felt self-conscious when she was on-line. Until now, that is, when Flash reminded her that she wasn't really Blondie.

At least you deserve an answer, Holly thought. She spread her fingers out over her keyboard.

Then she froze. *But what's it going to be? I'm going to have to make a decision sooner or later.*

Just then Holly heard a knock on her door. *I guess that means later,* she mused to herself.

"Come in!" she called out, turning in time to see Eileen's freckled face poking into her room.

"Hi," Eileen said brightly. "I got a message that you wanted to talk to me about something?"

"Oh, right," Holly said. "It's about Club Z."

"Oh," Eileen said.

"I don't know if anyone mentioned it to you yesterday," Holly began. "We're all wondering about how we get in tonight. Are there actual invitations? Or just a guest list or something?"

Holly saw the frozen smile on Eileen's face and paused. "Eileen?" Holly asked. "The Kappas *are* invited, aren't they? That's what Soozie said, though I don't always take her word for everything. I just thought—"

"No, no," Eileen interrupted. "I'm on my way to see Emmet right now."

"Great!" Holly smiled. She couldn't wait to see the new club.

"Don't tell me you're doing work on a Friday morning?" Eileen asked, nodding at the computer.

"Nope," Holly replied. "I'm on-line right now." She pointed to the box on her computer screen where the message from Flash was still spread across the monitor. "That's a note from the guy I was telling you about."

"The one from the arts newsgroup?" Eileen asked, suddenly interested. "And what's his name? Flash? That's cute."

"Yeah." Holly smiled. "And I'm Blondie. Not too original, but it works."

"Hey, he wants to meet you in person," Eileen said, pointing at the message. "That's great!"

"I guess," Holly muttered, chewing her lip.

"You don't sound too excited," Eileen said. "I thought you really liked this guy."

"I do," Holly said. "And he's told me how special he thinks I am."

"Really?" Eileen asked, smiling.

Holly knew she was blushing but she couldn't help it. She thought Flash was pretty special himself, and she couldn't deny there was something so romantic about it all.

"It's like he's a secret admirer that you get to communicate with," Eileen said.

"Exactly!" Holly replied, glad that someone else understood. "I mean, we've told each other some really personal things, and he seems just great."

"So why not meet him?" Eileen wondered.

"I guess I'm afraid of ruining what we have. What if we get along great as on-line buddies, but hate each other in person? Or what if he's just a total weirdo?"

"Holly," Eileen said. "Don't you think he's wondered about all these things, too?"

"I guess so," Holly admitted. "But I'm not a weirdo."

"Sure, but Flash doesn't know that, does he? And he's willing to meet you, isn't he? So give him the same chance he's giving you."

"You sound awfully wise all of a sudden," Holly teased. "But weren't you the one a few weeks ago who didn't want to give a certain Mr. Emmet Lehman another chance?"

Eileen chuckled. "Which qualifies me for the stupid prize of the year, which is why I'm saying this. Besides, this guy goes to Wilder, doesn't he? How bad could he be? I mean, you've already got a crush on him and you've never even seen him."

Holly shrugged, embarrassed. "I'll have to think about it some more before I answer."

"Trust your instincts," Eileen suggested.

"Maybe he'll be at Club Z tonight, too?" Holly wondered suddenly.

"Maybe you'd better plan on another date," Eileen murmured.

Holly nodded. "We probably shouldn't meet the first time at a huge crowded place. Tonight's reserved strictly for partying."

"Let's hope so," Eileen added.


"A cup of coffee, please," Nancy said, ignoring the menu the waitress left on the table. She was sitting at a booth in the Purity Coffee Shop in downtown Weston.

"Any lunch?" the waitress asked.

"No thanks"—Nancy squinted expectantly at the petite waitress's nametag—"Joan."

Nancy watched the waitress, who had short reddish hair and tiny features, as she poured a cup of coffee.

"Here you go," Joan said, leaving a thick mug of coffee and turning to go.

"I wonder if there is something you can help me with," Nancy said quickly. "Do you know Liana Schmidt?"

Joan looked at her suspiciously, then nodded hesitantly. "She used to work here."

"But she left after the Cal Evanson thing, right?"

Joan shifted on her feet. "You from the police or something?"

Nancy shook her head.

"Wait," Joan interjected, shooting Nancy a cold stare. "You're not working for Evanson's new lawyer, are you?"

"Not at all," Nancy said quickly. "I'm a reporter writing about the case."

"Oh," Joan said.

"I really wanted to talk to Liana."

"Who doesn't?" Joan replied icily. "Everybody's been calling. But she moved to another part of town and didn't exactly advertise her new address. Her number's unlisted, so don't bother calling directory assistance. If you ask me, I don't blame her."

"Me neither," Nancy replied sympathetically.

"What happened was terrible. Were you here then?"

Joan gave a slight nod. Nancy could see that she had been asked the same question dozens of times and was tired of the attention. And Joan seemed a little afraid. But who wouldn't be? Cal Evanson—or the real attacker—was still out there.

"Did you know Evanson?" Nancy asked.

Joan nodded, then shook her head mournfully. "He was a regular here," she said. "At first we all thought he was a nice guy. He used to flirt with Liana and me. But then I started to think there was something different about him, know what I mean? I got weird vibes from him, and after a while, I figured maybe he wasn't such a nice guy. I wasn't surprised to hear that he was capable of doing those things."

Nancy was listening intently. "Can you be more specific?"

Suddenly Joan's eyes widened. "You're not going to write that I said any of this, are you? Because that creep is walking the streets now, and if he heard I said anything—"

Nancy held up her hand. "Don't worry. I won't quote you. I'm really more interested in the personal angle of the case."

"Yeah, well, aren't we all," Joan said coldly, and started to back away. "I could use a cigarette . . ."

"Could I talk to you again?" Nancy called after her.

Joan didn't answer. She disappeared into the kitchen.

Lost in thought, Nancy finished her coffee, left a dollar, and got up to leave.

I'm not surprised she's afraid to talk, Nancy mused as she headed for the door. I'd be, too. But I wonder how she came to all these conclusions about Cal Evanson?

Outside, the sun was blindingly bright, and Nancy had to shield her eyes. As she headed for her Mustang, she couldn't really see and bumped into a large, dark-haired man getting out of a green sedan.

"Oh, sorry," Nancy said.

The man just scowled and grumbled under his breath.

"Have a nice day," Nancy muttered to herself.

About to duck into her car, Nancy stopped. Joan had come around from the back of the diner and was waving to the guy Nancy had bumped.

"Hey, Larry," she called affectionately. "It's been a long time. Where've you been keeping yourself?"

Well, she's in a better mood, Nancy thought. She twisted the key in the ignition, and her car roared to life.

Everyone's so sure he's guilty, she mused. And maybe he is . . . She twisted around and started to back out. Or maybe he's not."

\* \* \*

"I just couldn't tell her," Eileen said, leaning over the table at Java Joe's. The campus coffee shop was full and buzzing with excitement about the upcoming weekend. "I tried. I really did. I mean, I dropped some hints—"

"You're saying they *still* think they're coming?" Emmet asked, his eyes wide.

Eileen just nodded.

"*All* of them?" Emmet asked.

Eileen nodded again. "What could I say? They're sorority sisters."

"Well, Jason told me again a little while ago there's no way he's going to invite even one more person," Emmet said, "let alone an entire sorority."

"They're going to murder me," Eileen said under her breath.

"Anyway"—Emmet smiled—"we're going. And I hope you're prepared to have an amazing time."

"Hmmm," Eileen could only murmur. Emmet was lightly stroking her hand. "Amazing," she purred, staring lovingly into the warm eyes of her boyfriend.

"And until then—" Emmet began.

"No more Club Z?" Eileen begged.

"What do you mean no Club Z!" Kara Verbeck cried from over Eileen's shoulder. "Does that mean the club isn't opening? What's wrong?"

Eileen looked up to see Kara standing by their

table with two of Kara's sisters from the Pi Phi sorority, Nikki Bennett and Montana Smith.

"There's nothing wrong with the club," Emmet said.

"We were just hoping *not* to talk about it for a while." Eileen sighed.

"Why wouldn't you want to talk about it?" Kara asked excitedly. "The opening of a new club is totally exciting."

"And," Montana added, tossing her blond, corkscrew hair, "big events always need publicity."

"Would this have anything to do with your radio show?" Eileen asked.

Kara, Nikki, and Montana were the hosts of a weekly show on the college radio station.

"Funny you should ask . . ." Nikki said with a giant grin.

"A radio interview with Jason Lehman would give Club Z lots of free publicity," Kara said.

"Not to mention the way we could plug it on-air during all our commercial breaks," Montana added.

"I'm just *sure* your brother would jump at the opportunity to talk about his plans for the club to a college audience," Kara finished.

"Well," Emmet was saying, "I guess I could ask him—"

"Why don't you let us ask him?" Nikki interrupted.

"Say, tonight?" Kara suggested.

"At the Club Z opening?" Montana added.

Is there anyone who doesn't want an invitation? Eileen thought to herself.

"The guest list is really full," Emmet explained. "I don't think anybody else—"

"But, Eileen," Kara pleaded, "I'm one of your own suitemates. Weren't you going to get everyone from our suite into the opening?"

"And what about two of your own suitemate's best friends?" Montana nudged Kara in the side.

"She really can't—" Emmet started to say.

"I'll see what I can do," Eileen added quickly. She felt guilty as soon as she saw the way their faces lit up.

"Really?" Kara asked, eyes bright with excitement. "You'll let us know?"

"We'll try," Eileen said, grinning as she kicked Emmet under the table.

"Uh, sure," Emmet blurted out. "We'll do what we can."

Kara smiled. "Great! If Jason does an interview with us, he won't regret it. Maybe we can even do it live."

Eileen waved goodbye as Kara, Nikki, and Montana left Java Joe's. She could hardly bring herself to meet Emmet's gaze.

"Eileen," he said threateningly.

"I know, I know." Eileen sighed, closing her eyes. "I just don't want to let anyone down."

"But, Eileen," Emmet said, "your friends will

be a lot more disappointed now that you've promised to get them in."

Eileen knew it was crazy, but she was still hoping something would happen. Just a small miracle. Jason had to change his mind—or she would never be forgiven!

"I just spent six dollars on lunch, and I don't feel as though I've eaten a thing," Stephanie said as she and Casey left the Student Union and started across the quad.

"Well, I'm stuffed," Casey replied.

Stephanie plucked a cigarette from her purse and rested it between her lips.

"You should try to stop smoking so many of those things," Casey said, snatching Stephanie's cigarette, extinguishing it, and tossing it into a trash can.

Stephanie sighed. "Look, I can't change my dating *and* smoking habits all in one day. I will never be Miss Princess Perfect, the Girl Who Can Do No Wrong."

Casey held up an admonishing finger. "But you can try."

Stephanie smiled bravely and slipped her lighter back in her purse. "I suppose I can."

A pair of drop-dead gorgeous men sauntered by, and Stephanie couldn't help noticing the expressions on their faces or where their eyes roamed as they passed. A small smile played across her face. She knew she and Casey were both hot. She was dark and mysterious, and Casey was all redheaded glamour.

Why shouldn't I enjoy the attention? Stephanie wondered. Isn't this what college is all about?

"Look, but don't touch," Casey warned her, as if she'd read Stephanie's mind.

"I'm sure I don't know what you mean," Stephanie replied, all innocence and light.

Casey's smile was not unkind. "Oh, yes, you do. Letting other men get under your skin is good for the ego. But it's all downhill after that. Unless you're in love. I've seen enough men in my life to know that Jonathan's worth your loyalty. Trust me."

"Okay, okay," Stephanie said, holding up her hands. "I see your point."

"Good. Because here comes your first test. I'm already late for Russian lit, so I'm out of here. Good luck."

Stephanie looked up to find Glen jogging toward her from across the quad.

"Casey," Stephanie pleaded. "After everything I told you about what happened, you're going to leave me alone with him?"

Casey wriggled her fingers goodbye. "You're on your own, Steph," she said. "If what you told Jonathan was true, and you really do love him, then this should be a piece of cake. You know what to do."

As Casey disappeared into a building, Glen's

large shadow passed in front of Stephanie. She squinted up into his face. "Hi," she said flatly.

"So I hope you ironed things out yesterday," Glen said, smiling the same arrogant smile.

"I did," Stephanie replied confidently. "I noticed you made your quick escape. You're good at that, aren't you?"

"No better than you," Glen replied craftily. He leaned closer. "So now we're free to go on a real date?"

Stephanie took a step back. "Look, Glen, Jonathan is my boyfriend. What happened yesterday"—she cleared her throat—"that kissing thing, was one time only. It won't happen again."

But Glen was still smiling. "Is that what you told your boyfriend?"

"It's what I'm telling you," she said forcefully.

"Well, your math needs a little help. If my memory serves me correctly, we kissed *twice*, not once."

Suddenly the image of the football game and Glen's arms and the sensation of his lips on hers came flooding back. Stephanie touched her forehead. She was beginning to get a very bad headache.

"Whatever," she said irritably. "But it's not going to happen again."

"Who are you fooling?" Glen laughed. "You're not a one-guy kind of girl, if you know what I mean. Anyone can see that—"

It was more an instinct than a decision. Before

she knew it, Stephanie's hand came up and slapped Glen's cheek—hard.

"I know what I am," she fumed, her throat tight with anger.

Stunned into silence, Glen worked his jaw. Stephanie had a thousand things she could say to him about her relationship with Jonathan, but none of them were any of his business.

Without another word, she stepped aside and breezed by him, ignoring the amused stares from the small crowd of students gathered on the walk.

Stephanie half-walked, half-ran back to Thayer Hall. All the way a little voice whispered in her ear—what you feel for Jonathan goes way beyond the cheap thrill of a creep like Glen. Glen could be any good-looking guy. Glen or Mike or Bill—they're all the same. Here one night and gone the next. But Jonathan is unique. He wants more than your body. He wants *you*. He loves you.

"Why do other people have such a hard time getting that through their heads?" Stephanie cried. "Why can't I?"

# CHAPTER 5

And in addition to the reporters on the *Chicago Tribune*, I've gotten calls from a number of colleagues on newspapers around the country," Steve Shapiro said as Nancy and the rest of the *Wilder Times* staff listened. "They're intrigued by Gail's story, and all say that no matter how much pressure the DA puts on her, she shouldn't give in."

Nancy gave Jake a look as Steve continued. "The fight to protect the identity of your sources is one of the toughest a journalist will ever fight."

Nancy had always admired Steve. As faculty advisor on the paper, he urged his students to chase down their stories instead of interviewing people over the phone.

"So what is the DA saying about Gail right now?" Nancy asked.

"I haven't been subpoenaed—yet," Gail replied. "My lawyer says that the DA wants to avoid a showdown in court that could end up with my going to jail."

"Just more bad publicity," Jake suggested.

"Exactly," Gail replied. "So they want me to come forward on my own with my source's name."

"You should also know," Steve added, "that a number of Wilder board members have pressed Gail to give in. But she's holding her ground, like a pro."

This is so amazing, Nancy thought to herself. All of this national attention focused on the Wilder campus newspaper. She tried to get Jake's attention across the room. Nancy knew he was finding this as exciting as she was.

"The DA tried to get me to give up the name," Gail continued, "by saying that he needs my source's testimony to secure the second conviction against Evanson. But I'm not buying it. If they're retrying Evanson, they have to feel they have enough evidence. I can't reveal this source, no matter how I feel about that guy."

"This morning Wilder's president called to give Gail his support," Steve added. "We've been getting phone calls supporting her from faculty and students all day."

"Should we table the other pieces on Evanson until this thing blows over?" Jake asked.

"Absolutely not," Steve insisted. "This paper

will not buckle under to pressure. Keep going, everybody."

The meeting broke up as Steve prepared to leave.

Gail motioned Nancy over. "I wanted to hear how your interview with Trisha Evanson went."

Nancy nodded. "We definitely need to talk—" she began. But before she could get very far, Steve cut in and stole Gail's attention as Nancy felt a hand on her arm, gently tugging her away.

"Pretty exciting, huh?" Jake whispered, taking a quick nibble on her ear.

Nancy nodded and smiled. Out of the corner of her eye, she noticed that Steve had left and Gail was alone, getting back to work at her desk. Nancy had to talk to her before she got involved in something else. She gave Jake's hand a squeeze. "Just a second . . ."

"So how did your assignment go?" Gail asked.

"Trisha's impressive," Nancy replied. "A great interview."

"Did she tell you anything new?" Gail asked.

"That's what I wanted to talk to you about. I want to shift the focus of my article a little. I read over the notes that Evanson's new lawyer made, and there's a possibility that Evanson's actually innocent."

"So his sister says," Gail said dismissively.

"No," Nancy corrected her, "so the notes from the new lawyer suggest."

Gail slowly raised her head. "Nancy, of course

Evanson's lawyer has notes indicating that Evanson is innocent. He's defending the guy."

"But—"

"Stick to the human interest story on the sister," Gail cut in.

"But I already talked to a waitress down at the Purity who worked with Liana Schmidt and knew Cal."

"Who?" Gail demanded to know.

"Her name was Joan. I didn't get her last name."

Gail fiddled distractedly with some papers on her desk. "You're still a novice reporter, Nancy. You didn't even get a full name on an interview subject. Stay with the assignment you've been given," she snapped.

Nancy tossed Jake an SOS, but he just shrugged. "But what about the new angle?" she asked.

Gail's expression became irritated. "Everything I've seen so far, and Steve agrees with me, supports the theory that Cal Evanson *is* the attacker," she stated evenly. "Why would you want to prove me wrong?"

Nancy shook her head. "I'm not trying to prove you wrong. But isn't that what we're supposed to do, report all sides of the story objectively and let the readers decide?"

Nancy could see frustration in Gail's face. "Look, I'm not trying to butt in on your story,

Gail," she said. "But there's new evidence, like that ring found in Evanson's apartment—"

"Nancy, you're not experienced enough to handle the tougher journalistic aspects of this story," Gail interrupted her again. "We're getting *national* attention on this story, and I'm already under tremendous pressure from the DA. I can't afford to make things any worse. Stay with the sister story. It's what's interesting to Wilder readers, since she *is* a Wilder student."

Nancy cocked her head in disbelief. "I'm not experienced enough? After all the stories I've done?"

Gail looked up at Jake and smiled. "She *is* ambitious. Look, guys, I have a thousand things to do. So, is everything straightened out?"

Without answering, Nancy gathered her notes and walked out of the office. Needing a breath of fresh air, she headed down the stairs for the quad. Jake followed.

"Can you believe that?" Nancy fumed when she and Jake were alone. "I'm onto a potentially ground-breaking lead, and Gail says I can't handle it!"

Jake kicked at a pebble. "I don't know, Nance. I sort of agree with Gail."

Nancy stared at him in dumbfounded silence. "You what? How *could* you agree with Gail?"

Jake shrugged. "She asked you to cover one angle, and now you're covering another. Somebody has to do the human interest side."

Amazed, Nancy narrowed her eyes. Was this Jake Collins, the journalistic cowboy, talking?

"I can't believe you're saying this." She seethed quietly.

Jake stepped forward and reached for her arm. "You're a great journalist, but an order is—"

He couldn't finish, so Nancy finished for him. "An order?" Shaking her head, she laughed ruefully. "It's like I don't even know who you are."

Not bothering to retrieve her jacket and books from upstairs, Nancy threw up her hands, turned, and headed for her car.

"What about tonight, Club Z?" Jake called after her.

"Forget about tonight," she snapped.

"If you weren't helping me with biology, I don't know what I'd be doing," Bess said as she finally closed her book after a major study session with Ginny Yuen, one of Nancy's suitemates.

"You've been getting good grades all year," Ginny replied. "I'm glad I can help, but you're actually a better student than you think."

"Maybe," Bess said. "But missing so much school after the accident has set me back."

Smiling, Ginny slid her own notebooks into her bag. "You didn't miss that much while you were home recovering."

Bess grimaced inside. But she was grateful that Ginny wasn't tiptoeing around her, trying not to bring up the subject of the accident.

"Are you done studying yet?" Janie Covington asked, popping her white blond head into the Kappa living room.

Bess smiled at her sorority sister. "We're done."

Janie, Soozie, and a few other Kappa upperclassmen plopped down on the couches.

"We need to mellow out and save our energy for tonight's party at Club Z," Janie said.

"That's if Eileen doesn't let us down," Soozie warned ominously.

"I'm sure she won't," Bess replied. "She would have said something by now if we couldn't go."

"She told me a few hours ago that everything was going to be fine," Holly said as she came in.

"Ahh, look who's here," Bess joked, smiling at Holly. "The cyber-hitchhiker of love!"

"Hardly," Holly replied, waving her hand.

"She's been surfing the Internet looking for love," Bess informed Ginny.

"What she really means," Holly clarified, "is that I've been going on-line and chatting with people."

"So how do you meet someone?" Ginny asked.

"They have these Usenet groups for all different topics and interests," Holly said. "You go to one that you like, and you automatically have something in common with whoever else is there. I met Flash in an arts group."

"Flash?" Soozie sneered, rolling her eyes.

"He likes to run," Holly replied. "And that's what his running buddies call him."

"Well, it's a pretty stupid name if you ask me," Soozie said.

"Lucky nobody asked then, isn't it?" Janie shot back acidly.

Bess had to hold back a chuckle. Soozie and Janie were almost as deadly rivals as Soozie and Holly, and never missed an opportunity to snipe.

"And what do *you* call yourself?" Ginny asked.

"Blondie," Holly answered. "And in case you want to know, Soozie, it's Blondie, for blond hair."

Soozie sniffed. "How original."

"It sounds fun!" Bess said. "You can be whoever you want to be."

"The point is to be yourself," Holly said. "That's what makes it work. You have the freedom to be totally honest. That's why it's a big decision to think about meeting for real."

"What do you mean, for real?" Bess asked.

"Flash wants to meet in person," Holly admitted. "And I'm thinking about saying yes."

"I wonder what it's like to be so desperate that you'd actually consider a date with a guy who calls himself Flash," Soozie said airily, addressing no one in particular. Then she looked at Holly and sneered. "If he's so wonderful, why does he need to hide behind a computer screen? He's probably a dork."

Janie glared at her. "Do you try to be cruel, or does it come naturally?"

"It's okay," Holly replied good-naturedly. "It's not a way to hide, Soozie. It's the opposite. It's a way to meet people who actually share your interests. People you might never run into otherwise."

Bess tried to imagine agreeing to meet someone she'd only talked to over the computer. It seemed intriguing. And dangerous. Then again, it was just like going on a blind date. Or making a date with someone you just met.

In fact, before she'd gotten to know Paul, all Bess knew about him was that he was willing to make a complete fool of himself by serenading her under her window in the dorm. And he'd turned out to be wonderful.

"Well," Bess said thoughtfully, "I guess he could be awful." Her eyes lit up. "But he could also be fabulous!"

"Fat chance," Soozie grumbled.

"Well, even if he's not exactly the same as you," Ginny offered, "you could still have a great relationship. You may discover new things about yourself with this guy."

Bess knew that Ginny was talking about her relationship with her ex-boyfriend, Ray Johansson. Ginny had discovered a talent for songwriting when she'd been with the sexy rocker musician.

"I have to write him back soon and tell him what I've decided," Holly said.

"Well, don't think about it until tomorrow," Bess warned. "Tonight it's party time at Club Z!"

"I can hardly wait until Sunday," Pam said excitedly to Jesse as they sat in a small booth at Java Joe's. Jesse had just finished explaining to Pam all the preparations he was making for Saturday night's party and Sunday's announcement of the Midwest winner in the Natural Shades modeling contest.

"Oh, sure you can"—Jesse winked—"it'll be worth it, I'm sure. You did have fun during your interviews, didn't you?"

"Of course I did," Pam replied. "I felt like a totally different person after my makeover."

"Well, maybe you should get used to that feeling," Jesse suggested, sipping his coffee.

Pam could hardly contain herself. So far in their conversation, Jesse had made a number of remarks like that. It definitely sounded to her as if he were dropping some strong hints that she was actually the winner!

"You really think so?" Pam asked.

"Oh, sure," Jesse replied. "And I bet you'd love it," he said, "being able to travel the world with Natural Shades. And with me."

It was exciting to think of winning the model search. But Jesse's effusive compliments were starting to put a damper on the idea. Pam had been careful since the beginning of their conversation to mention Jamal whenever she could, but Jesse didn't seem to be picking up on her signals. He knew she was unavailable, but that obviously wasn't stopping him from coming on to her.

*"Jamal* would be happy, too." Pam smiled, trying to remind Jesse of her boyfriend's existence without being rude. "I know he'd be proud of me. And he'd love to travel a little."

"Maybe he'd finally realize what a beautiful woman he has," Jesse said. "I certainly did."

"You were really supportive during the interviews," Pam said diplomatically.

"You don't think he takes you for granted?" Jesse asked. "I'd take you any way I could get you."

Pam almost didn't know how to reply. Jesse had gone from friendly, to flirtatious, to out-and-out slimy.

"Well," Pam muttered, knowing she was red with embarrassment, "that's very sweet—"

"Pam," Jesse said, leaning closer and taking her hand in his. "If you think that's sweet, there's a lot I could show you. And I'd really like to. Especially since we could be working together."

"Working together?"

"Well," Jesse said softly, "in just a few days I think you'll realize there'll be lots of opportunities to get to know me better." He paused and wrapped his fingers around Pam's wrist. Slowly he moved his hand up her arm.

"I just don't see why we should wait that long," Jesse added.

Lightly, Pam pulled her arm away. This was too much! It was exactly the kind of stuff Jamal had accused Jesse of before. And even though Jamal had been wrong then, it looked as if he'd been right about what kind of guy Jesse was.

"Promise to meet me later," Jesse said. He smiled, but now his smile seemed like a leer. Pam was getting the creeps.

"I'll be back at my motel room by nine tonight," Jesse said. "It would be a beautiful way to start a long friendship."

"I'm not so sure about that," Pam replied tightly.

"Don't be shy, Pam," Jesse said, stroking her arm again. "It would be much more pleasant for us to work together if we were *close* friends."

"I really have to leave," Pam muttered, twisting her arm out of his grasp.

"Pam?"

Pam looked up and a wave of relief swept over her as she saw George walking up to their table.

"George!" Pam said, a little too brightly. "You're finally here."

George acted confused.

"I was just stopping by—" George began.

"To pick me up for a meeting," Pam interrupted. "Which is only"—Pam checked her watch—"ten minutes from now."

"Meeting?" George asked, acting more confused.

"Yes, remember?" Pam said, giving George a long stare.

"Pam?" Jesse asked, reaching out to touch her

cheek, and then drawing his fingers along her arm. "Are you *sure* you have to leave now?"

"Yes," Pam said, jumping up from the table so fast she knocked her coffee cup over. "I have to go."

"Some other time, Pam," Jesse murmured. "Hopefully soon."

"What was that all about?" George asked as she and Pam left Java Joe's. "He had his hands all over you."

"I know." Pam shuddered. "Thank goodness you weren't Jamal, or it would have been an even uglier scene in there."

"Is that the guy from Natural Shades?" George asked.

"Yes," Pam replied. "You won't believe this, but he was hinting that I was the winner of the model search."

"Really!" George cried. "Pam, that's great!"

"Well," Pam said, "that was before he actually had the nerve to invite me to his motel room tonight."

"You're kidding," George replied. "How slimy!"

"Totally," Pam agreed.

"What a jerk," George said.

"A big jerk," Pam echoed.

But there was one thing Pam couldn't help thinking as they walked away: I just hope I haven't wrecked my chances of being the Natural Shades model.

# CHAPTER 6

Jake was slumped down in his chair at the newspaper. He'd spent the hour since Nancy had stormed out trying to work on his Evanson article.

He lifted his eyes to the monitor. At last count his ambitious story consisted of twelve whole sentences.

"She's driving me crazy," he groaned. A mental picture of Nancy in a happier moment, her crystal blue eyes glinting in the sun, floated by. "I need air."

Outside, Jake wandered through the chilly twilight toward Sage Field House.

"Shooting hoops is good medicine," he muttered as he pushed through the big double doors.

But he wasn't alone. George and her boyfriend, Will Blackfeather, were playing one-on-

one at a far basket. George, tall and graceful, and Will, powerfully built with raven black hair and high cheekbones, looked so awesome together. Nancy and I look great together, too, Jake thought, feeling suddenly wistful.

Breaking free of his thoughts, Jake jogged over to George and Will and clapped his hands for the ball. "Here!"

"Heads up," George cried, and fired a behind-the-back bounce pass. Jake caught it and took a long arcing jump shot.

"Nice touch," Will commented.

"If only I were that lucky with women," Jake lamented, making an obvious play for their pity.

Taking the bait, George rolled her eyes. "What is it now, Collins?" she asked.

"Nancy's your friend," he said. "You tell me."

"Actually, Nancy and I did talk about you yesterday," George admitted, "but I'm not sure she has any ideas either."

"Do you?"

"Personally," George replied offhandedly, "I don't think there's anything wrong."

Jake shook off his jean jacket and picked up the ball. "So if nothing's wrong," he asked, "why isn't it right? It's like every little thing that wouldn't have been a big deal a month ago is now a fight. First this thing with her dad and Avery. And today—"

"Today?" George prodded him.

Jake told them about the controversy over the

piece Nancy was writing. "I mean, Gail is in a very tough position," he explained. "She's been working hard to find out the facts for her story. And with all the publicity she has to make sure the paper doesn't print anything it can't back up."

Will pursed his lips. "But what does Nancy's story have to do with hers? You know Nancy wouldn't write anything she didn't have the facts to back up."

"True," Jake replied, "but Gail is also responsible for the pecking order at the paper. Nancy is a freshman. There are other reporters, including me, who should be handling the investigative side of this."

George, hands on hips, threw Jake a skeptical look. "That seems a bit unfair. She shouldn't do the story because she's a freshman reporter."

Jake shrugged. "That's newspaper politics."

George snatched the ball out of Jake's hands and sank a jump shot. "Then I don't blame Nancy for being mad."

"Seems to me," Will cut in, "that if you trust each other, this'll blow over and you'll come up with a way to work it out."

Trust each other. Jake pondered the thought. Maybe that's what's missing—trust. I have to show her how much she means to me.

"So Holly's doing some on-line dating?" Nancy asked as Bess was filling her in.

After her study session with Ginny, Bess had decided to pay Nancy a visit at her dorm. For some reason all the discussion about computer dating at the sorority was getting her down. And besides, it had been a while since she'd had a good long talk with Nancy.

"It's funny, isn't it?" Bess agreed. "I don't know why it should be. People meet in stranger ways."

"Yeah." Nancy chuckled. "It might actually be fun to meet someone on-line."

"I was thinking the same thing," Bess admitted. "It did sound like a kick. Although I just can't imagine talking to another guy without thinking of Paul." Bess sighed as she flopped down on Nancy's bed. "And now that I'm thinking of him, I'm starting to feel really nervous about the Zeta party on Saturday. Maybe it's too soon? Maybe I shouldn't go."

"It sounds like you're making excuses," Nancy said. "You don't need to feel guilty about having fun."

"I'm just scared that I'll lose it completely," Bess muttered. "It'll be the first time I've been back to Paul's frat house since—since he died," she finished softly.

"Don't worry, Bess," Nancy said, throwing a supportive arm around her. "We'll all be there with you. And it may be just the right place for you to have a great time—surrounded by all the people who knew and loved him."

"That's true." Bess nodded. It was a good way to think about it, and suddenly Bess actually felt a little excited about the Zeta party. It *would* be a good way to celebrate Paul—to remember him among his friends.

"And while we're on the subject of parties," Nancy said, grinning, "aren't you going to Club Z tonight? I figured all the Kappas would be there."

"Along with you, I hope," Bess said.

"Everyone else in the suite seems to think so," Nancy agreed. "Although we don't have any official invitations yet."

"Well, for Eileen's sake I hope these elusive invitations show up, or she'll be on Soozie's hit list. But at least it will get Soozie off *my* back for a while," Bess added with a grin. "So what about this big criminal case coming up? George told me you're working on a big story."

"I am," Nancy replied. "And I was digging for some new angles on it, which isn't going over too well with my boyfriend. Or my editor."

"What do you mean?" Bess asked.

"I don't have any new facts about the case," Nancy admitted. "But I've talked to a number of people, and I'm beginning to get the feeling that this Cal Evanson may not be guilty."

"Wow!" Bess whistled.

Nancy nodded, and Bess could see her friend's blue eyes darken with worry, and something else. Anger.

"Both Gail and Jake almost bit my head off when I suggested changing my piece from a human interest story to an investigative one," Nancy said.

"That doesn't seem fair," Bess said. "Shouldn't you be pursuing every lead?"

"That's what I think," Nancy agreed. "And it's what I'm going to do even if neither of them wants me to."

"I hope it's not causing any trouble between you and Jake," Bess said softly.

Nancy smiled ruefully. "Usually, I find him so adorable it's hard to stay angry." Her expression turned pensive as she stared out the window. "But for some reason I'm not getting over this one so quickly."

"You will," Bess replied breezily.

She pulled herself off Nancy's bed and grabbed her jacket. "Well, I guess I should go."

As Bess and Nancy walked by the lounge, they found Ginny talking with Liz and Jenny.

"Ginny was just telling us about the computer couple, Blondie and Flash." Liz giggled. "What a way to date!"

"We *are* heading into the twenty-first century," Nancy joked.

"Unfortunately," Liz said happily, "I already have a fabulous boyfriend so I won't be able to experience my own cyber-romance."

"I'm so busy right now I wouldn't even have the time for a computer," Jenny said.

Everyone was laughing when the door to the suite flew open.

"I just saw Eileen and Emmet," Reva Ross said, blowing into the lounge like a tornado. Bess noticed Reva was glowing with excitement. "I don't know what happened, but Eileen said that Jason finally surrendered. He's letting Eileen and Emmet put all their friends on the guest list. As long as we can fit in the front door—we're in!"

All the girls in the lounge whooped with excitement. All except Jenny, that is.

"Oh, great," Jenny moaned. "I was hoping that if Liz couldn't go to the party, I'd be able to convince her to come to Rand Hall instead."

"And work on a Friday night?" Bess asked, aghast.

"It's not that unusual for architect students," Liz pointed out.

"The only unusual thing is that Liz finished her project ahead of schedule," Jenny said, making a face at her friend. "So now, after a gloriously dull evening waitressing at the Bumblebee Diner, I'll have to spend the rest of the night slaving away at my desk in the studio."

"That's too bad," Bess said sympathetically.

"Yeah," Ginny agreed.

"A real bummer," Liz added.

"Tough luck," Reva said.

"What a drag," Nancy offered.

There was silence for a moment, and then they all burst out laughing.

"Oh, thanks very much," Jenny cried, trying to keep herself from laughing, too. "Way to make me feel better. I hope you all have a terrible time. Club Z? Zzzzzzz . . ." Jenny snored.

Bess turned and grabbed Nancy by the arm. She was feeling better after their talk, and now the idea of a night of fun and excitement was just what she needed.

"Come on, Nan!" Bess cried, pulling her back down the hall to Nancy's room. "We've got a party in a few hours, and I have to figure out what I can borrow of yours to wear!"

"Thank you for coming, Ms. Gardeski. We'll keep this brief and to the point. . . . We can't support . . . can't support . . . can't support . . ."

Gail was on her way home from campus, trying to get there as fast as she could. Now she waited at an intersection. Red light, green light, red light again. The cars were honking, but she couldn't move. Her eyes glazed over, and all she could see was the long mahogany table in the boardroom of the Wilder University trustees and the stern, hostile faces of the trustees themselves. The booming voice of the chair was still echoing in her head an hour later. "We can't support . . ."

Just after the staff meeting at the *Times* broke up, the secretary for the Chair of the Wilder Board of Trustees had called her and Steve Shapiro in for a conference. The upshot of the meeting was that the board felt Gail was embarrassing the university and that they felt the DA deserved her cooperation. Gail winced as she remembered the anger in the chairman's voice as he said that alumni were calling to complain.

"We have let the president know that we do not support your position," he'd said. He reminded her that she was still just a student on the newspaper. She was not a professional reporter on a commercial paper.

Very carefully, very professionally, she thought, she'd told them that she was obligated to stand her ground. That the first amendment of the U.S. Constitution supported her position. That if she had to, she'd go to jail. She wouldn't be the first journalist to do it or the last.

They didn't take it well.

And now here she sat at the red light, feeling their warning ring like a slap across her face.

Finally Gail blinked to life and started driving again. "What a nightmare," she whispered. "Maybe I'll switch my major to something safe like marine biology."

As she was passing the neighborhood video store, Gail suddenly pulled in and sat breathing heavily in the parking lot.

"I have to escape for a while," she told herself. "I need to find something to take my mind off all of this."

She saw in her head what she wanted to do— hole up in her apartment, change into sweats, cradle a pint of ice cream in her lap, kick the phone off the hook, and watch a movie. Earlier she'd called her answering machine for messages. There were twenty. She decided not to answer a single one. Not tonight.

Inside the store, Gail wandered up and down the aisles, waiting for a movie to jump out at her. There were thousands of them: comedies, dramas, cartoons, musicals. But she couldn't make another decision, even one as small as this.

Closing her eyes, she was about to reach for a box, any box, when a voice invaded her peace.

"Gail? Gail Gardeski?"

Gail squinted. The lovely face was all too familiar: the creamy complexion, soft hazel eyes, and dark hair.

Oh, no. Is this a nightmare, she wondered, or is this real?

But Gail saw the name tag on the girl standing in front of her: Liana Schmidt. This was no dream.

"I saw you on the news last night," Liana said.

"You work here?" Gail asked.

Liana nodded. "I left the coffee shop after the trial. I thought I told you that when we talked?"

"Right, sorry," Gail said, smiling uncomfortably. "I've been so busy. . . ."

Liana's expression was anything but pleasant. Her mouth was a grim line, and her black eyes smoldered with anger. "Just out of curiosity, have *you* ever been attacked or molested?" she asked matter-of-factly.

Gail could only shake her head.

"Do you know how afraid I am every night, knowing that animal is back on the streets?"

Again, Gail didn't have an answer.

Liana leveled a stiff finger at Gail. "Your source could put Cal Evanson back in jail for good. But you won't tell anyone who it is. Now he'll go free and terrorize this community all over again."

"He'll be convicted again," Gail implored her. "I'm sure of it."

"If he's not and he attacks someone," Liana said tightly. "I just hope *you* can live with that."

# CHAPTER 7

**I**'m glad you called me." Nancy clutched the steering wheel of her car.

"And I'm relieved you said yes," Jake replied softly from the passenger seat. He uncurled her hands from the wheel and brought them to his lips.

Nancy smiled, realizing just how much she wanted them to be together. She'd dressed for the occasion, not just for the club opening, but also to impress Jake. Over tight black jeans, she wore a slinky coffee-colored shirt that hugged her figure and set off her blue eyes.

After getting out of the car, they walked arm in arm through the chill air toward the club. The night was the perfect backdrop for romance: clear and starry. And in his black linen blazer and white T-shirt, Jake was the image of sexy sophistication.

"It looks amazing!" Nancy said enthusiastically as the club came into view.

The club was set in the old warehouse district with its long rows of huge brick buildings. The club, the first floor of an old factory, had a black-and-silver awning over the door. Inside, the club was breathtakingly electric.

Nancy and Jake opened the door to a tidal wave of sound and excitement. The cavernous eggplant-colored space had a long stage against one wall, where a four-piece local rock band was playing. Across the wood dance floor stretched a beautiful bar and a grill area where you could buy snacks. Suspended by long cables above it was a system of metal platforms connected by staircases, where people were sitting and talking, and even dancing. Over a sea of bobbing dancers, dozens of steel ceiling fans spun like propellers, and a hundred Z-shaped neon lights shone like pieces of lightning.

"Isn't this cool?"

Nancy whirled around. Reva was dancing in place, her slinky figure glimmering in a long black dress.

"You look great!" Nancy cried above the noise.

"Doesn't she?" said a guy standing next to her. But it wasn't Reva's boyfriend, Andy Rodriguez.

Reva smiled at the guy's compliment. Tall, and much older, in his double-breasted suit the guy seemed to be out of place. Reva pointed at him.

"This is Jesse Potter. He's the rep from Natural Shades Cosmetics." Reva threw Nancy a big wink.

Getting the point, Nancy smiled and held out her hand. "Hi. But where's Andy?" she asked.

"Sick."

"Conveniently," Nancy replied mischievously, and raised her eyebrows. "So, Jesse, is Reva's face going to be plastered all over America?"

Smiling handsomely, Jesse zipped his fingers across his mouth. "My lips are sealed," he said.

Nancy poked Reva in the side. "You're *it!* Look at him, he can't take his eyes off you," she whispered excitedly.

Reva grinned from ear to ear. "I know!"

"Hey, there's everyone from our suite!" Nancy cried, pointing to a cocktail table on one of the platforms overhead. Stephanie was standing to the side looking sultry in a silk spaghetti-string minidress. But she was alone and seemed to be unhappy as she stood scanning the crowd.

"Where's Jonathan?" Nancy raised her head toward Stephanie.

Reva shrugged. "Over an hour late."

Nancy raised an eyebrow. "He better hurry up," she quipped. "Guys are going to start migrating toward her."

Everyone had raised a glass and was waving for them to come up.

"You want to?" Jake asked, obviously disappointed.

Nancy grinned broadly. "No way! I want to dance!"

Jake took her by the waist. "Well, then, put your money where your mouth is."

Feeling her adrenaline pump, Nancy tossed her hair over her shoulder, clutched Jake's hand, and tugged him toward the middle of the floor. In a few minutes, she was sweating and writhing to the driving beat of the music and Jake's own rhythm. The rest of the world evaporated. They were a team again. They didn't need words or explanations or excuses to soothe things over. For the first time in days, she felt the indescribable passion that drew them together initially and helped her forget her old boyfriend from River Heights, Ned Nickerson.

Between songs, Jake, breathing heavily, leaned toward her and spoke, "I could use some air."

"But we just got here!" Nancy exclaimed.

"Come on," Jake insisted, pulling her toward the entrance.

On her way out, Nancy noticed something and slowed. Reva was standing on the highest of the platforms, near the ceiling, not looking too happy. Jesse Potter had his arm around her waist. Twisting away from him, Reva said something over her shoulder and unpeeled his arm.

"Not cool," Nancy commented. But Jake had her outside before she could think about it.

"What is it?" Nancy asked, half-annoyed at being torn away from the excitement. But the expectant look on Jake's face softened her up. "Okay," she said with a loving smile, "what?"

"This." Jake pulled out of his jacket pocket a box with Weston Jewelers embossed in gold on the front.

"Jake?" she asked quizzically.

A memory flashed in front of her. The summer before she'd left for college, Ned had taken her out to dinner. In the parking lot of the restaurant he'd handed her a box just like this one. Inside it was a locket. "So you won't forget," Ned had said.

"It's so you won't forget," Jake was saying.

Nancy looked up, alarmed and confused. "What?" she asked.

"That I always love you," Jake added. "No matter what."

Carefully, Nancy opened the box. Inside lay a stunning, fragile gold chain studded with delicate rose and black gemstones.

"Oh, Jake!" she said, and circled her arms around his neck. "I love it," she whispered in his ear. "You're so wonderful!"

"I want to make this relationship work," he said emotionally but firmly.

"I know. I'm sorry for all the tension. For letting this case get between us."

Jake picked the necklace out of the box and strung it gently around her neck. "It looks beautiful on you."

Looking down, Nancy fingered the necklace and blinked. Here was Jake standing in front of her: strong and talented and handsome. But the word *Ned* was on her lips. She swallowed it down. This was all too weird!

It's Jake, and he's telling you how much he cares for you, Nancy reminded herself. Then why am I thinking about Ned?

Gritting her teeth, she shook all that away. *This* is my life now, she persisted. I'm with *Jake*.

She wiped her hand over her face. What's wrong with me?

Determined, Nancy grabbed Jake by the hand and headed back toward the club entrance. "Come on. Nothing's going to get in our way tonight!"

"This is unbelievable," Emmet said, looking around the packed club. "Jason must be making a killing!"

"It's looking pretty successful," Eileen agreed happily. "So, how does it feel to be in the night club business, Mr. Lehman Junior?"

"Oh, well, hmm"—Emmet straightened his jacket and spread his arms—"it's terrific, just terrific. The loud music, the wild partying."

He grabbed Eileen and pulled her into his arms. "And, Ms. O'Connor, how does it feel to be in the arms of Mr. Lehman?"

"Fabulous," Eileen said happily. "Just fabulous. The rock hard muscles, the wild heartbeat. And the late nights . . ."

"Most definitely the late nights," Emmet agreed, whispering in her ear.

"You know," Eileen said, resting her head against Emmet's chest, "this party is incredible. And it's great to be here, especially after being harassed about it all week and worrying if I was going to be kicked out of my suite and my sorority for letting down my friends."

"I've heard that tone of voice before," Emmet teased, putting his warm hand on the back of Eileen's neck.

"But," Eileen murmured, "there is actually someplace I'd rather be instead of here with you in the middle of a crowded party."

"And where is that?" Emmet asked.

"Alone with you," Eileen admitted. "Anywhere else."

"Are you suggesting that we skip out on the big Club Z bash?" Emmet asked. "Miss the hottest event of the year?"

"Well," Eileen replied with a sigh, "when you put it like that . . ."

"It sounds like a great idea," Emmet agreed, a wicked grin curling his lips. Eileen watched happily as those lips came closer. She closed her eyes as Emmet kissed her and completely forgot she was crushed into a room with hundreds of people and a loud band.

"Let's get out of here," Emmet said breathlessly as he lifted his head. "To Club TwoEA."

"Which is?"

"Eileen and Emmet," he replied. "Alone."

\*      \*      \*

Usually Holly didn't spend all night at a party just checking out guys. Not that she wasn't interested, but it just wasn't her kind of thing. A lot of the other Kappas did, Kappas like Soozie and her friends who were standing near Holly and Janie at the edge of the dance floor.

But that night it seemed as if all the cutest guys on campus had found their way into Club Z, and Holly couldn't help wondering if Flash was one of them.

Is that whom I've been telling my secrets to? she thought as she caught a glimpse of a handsome guy with wavy black hair standing at the bar.

Or maybe it was the one with dark red hair wearing a white T-shirt, leaning against the stage?

"Excuse me?"

Holly felt a light tap on her shoulder. She turned around and found herself looking into the pale brown eyes of a very attractive guy.

Flash? Holly wondered.

"I'm Ben," he said, holding out his hand.

"Oh, hi." Holly couldn't help sounding disappointed.

"Are you expecting someone else?" Ben asked.

"No, no, I'm sorry," Holly apologized. "My name's Holly."

"Well, Holly"—Ben smiled, motioning to the raucous crowd on the dance floor—"would you like to dance?"

"I'd love to," Holly said quickly. At least if it

would stop her thinking about Flash. Holly took Ben's hand and they pushed their way into the wriggling crowd.

The house band started playing one of Holly's favorite songs. Ben turned out to be an excellent dancer, and for a few minutes Holly was able to forget about Flash and just enjoy herself.

Holly made eye contact with an adorable-looking blond guy who winked at her, and before Holly could stop herself she thought, Is *that* Flash?

Then it occurred to her that maybe Ben could be Flash.

"This is crazy," Holly muttered to herself, as the song finally came to an end and she followed Ben off the dance floor. She was thinking about Flash way too much. She had to do something about it.

"Thanks for the dance," Ben said, wiping the sweat from his forehead. "I don't think I've ever seen you on campus. What's your major?" he asked curiously.

"Art," Holly replied.

Ben nodded. "Well, that would explain it," he replied. "I'm in the engineering school." He shrugged apologetically. "I don't know too much about art," he admitted.

Strike out, Holly thought. Flash knew a lot about art.

"But I'd be willing to learn if you'd like to go out sometime?" Ben continued.

Immediately Holly felt a rush of pleasure. It

was always nice to be asked out and Ben was definitely cute. But to her own surprise, Holly realized she wasn't that interested in going out with Ben. She didn't know anything about him, but there *was* someone she did know a lot about, and suddenly Holly knew that's who she really wanted to date.

"Thanks for asking." Holly smiled sweetly. "But I'm sort of seeing someone already."

Even though I haven't actually laid eyes on him, Holly thought a little guiltily.

"Sorry to hear it." Ben blushed. "Thanks for the dance anyway."

As Holly watched Ben disappear into the crowd, her heart started beating faster. But it wasn't turning down Ben that made her pulse race, it was the thought of saying yes to Flash.

First thing in the morning, Holly would E-mail Flash.

"I guess it's time to finally get a look at the guy I'm seeing," Holly whispered to herself.

"This place is way cool," Ray said as they walked in under the neon purple sign. He'd come to the Club Z opening with Montana, Nikki, Kara, and Kara's boyfriend, Tim. Montana had invited him along as part of their group, but he had the feeling that she thought of it partly as a date.

Which, after checking out Montana, Ray had to admit wasn't such an awful idea. She was sexy with her riot of curly blond hair. He wasn't sure he was interested in starting up another relationship so soon after he and Ginny had broken up. In fact, Ray wasn't sure he even *wanted* another relationship if he couldn't be with Ginny.

But it was nice to hang out with someone, and Montana made it very easy for him. She was as opposite from Ginny as a person could get. And as far as Ray could tell, she had an extremely mellow personality.

"Wouldn't it be great to get Radical Moves to play here?" Montana asked, gazing around the enormous warehouse space. "This place is going to be the hottest club in Weston!"

Ray had to agree. Club Z was fantastic. The house band was in the middle of an instrumental jam, and Ray could tell that the sound system was top of the line.

"It's got a terrific setup for live music," Ray said. "This Lehman guy must know his stuff."

"We're still trying to get an interview with Jason," Kara told Ray.

"And if we get him on the show," Montana said, "we're going to make him listen to a tape of Radical Moves. I just know he's going to love you guys."

"I hope so," Ray said, suddenly thinking of the jam session they'd had the day before. Ray loved the band's sound, but still felt something was missing. He could only hope Jason Lehman didn't feel the same way.

"Why wouldn't he?" Nikki asked. "You guys are awesome."

"We're thinking of getting someone else in the band," Ray admitted. "Just to complete the sound."

"Another instrument?" Montana asked.

"Maybe," Ray replied, as the house band started its next number. "Or another voice."

Suddenly Ray's skin was tingling. Another voice, he realized. And I'm hearing it.

It was a woman who was singing. Her voice was rich and haunting. Ray turned to the house band and his jaw fell open in surprise.

"Karin?"

Ray couldn't believe it. It was Austin's old girl-friend—the reason Austin and Cory's old band had broken up. When they'd met, Ray had decided she was pretty rude, but he'd had no idea how unique her voice was.

As Ray listened, he knew that Karin's voice would be perfect for Radical Moves. It was exactly what the band was missing—something to complement his voice and distinctive enough to sound like another instrument.

"So, Ray," Montana said, leaning a little closer to him, "how about a dance?"

"What?" Ray asked, all his concentration on the band as their set came to an end. Karin smiled and thanked the crowd and explained that the band would be taking a ten-minute break.

Ray watched as she jumped off the stage and headed for the bar.

"I asked if you wanted to dance?" Montana repeated, her smile faltering just a little.

"I'm sorry," Ray said quickly, trying to keep his eyes on Karin as she threaded her way through the crowd, "but I'll be back in a minute."

Just as he turned away, Ray noticed the wounded expression on Montana's face and winced. He didn't mean to hurt her, but he just couldn't lose this opportunity to get to Karin. Her voice was just what Radical Moves needed!

"Thanks for cleaning up, Joe," Jenny said, as she balled up her apron and tossed it into a cabinet under the soda machine.

"No problem," the cook replied. "This was one of the slowest nights I've worked in years."

"There's a huge party at a new club downtown," Jenny explained. "That's where all the lucky people are."

"And you and me were stuck here all night?" Joe asked, gazing around at the empty booths of the Bumblebee Diner. "I guess that does make us the unlucky ones."

"I only wish my night was over," Jenny said. "I still have four hours of school work ahead of me."

"Tonight?" Joe cried. "But it's after eleven!"

"I'm just in time then," Jenny grumbled, pulling her jacket on and grabbing her bag of studio supplies.

"Walk safely," he called out. Jenny waved back from the front door.

The streets were quiet at this hour. Nobody was around. Jenny walked quickly and was just a few blocks from campus when an enormous dark shape leaped out from the far side of a car parked on a small side street.

Jenny started to run, but whoever it was got to her, grabbed her from behind, and clamped a gloved hand over her mouth. She felt her assailant tear her bag from her shoulder. Then he was grabbing at the buttons of her coat. She tried screaming, but the sound was muffled by the heavy gloves. All she could smell was old leather.

Suddenly the man whipped her around and grabbed her throat with one hand. Jenny found herself staring at a black ski mask. She watched in horror as his other hand reached out and ripped the necklace from her throat. Then the hand started down her chest. Terror filled her and she began thrashing wildly.

In her panic, she saw something pale flash in front of her for a second. It was his arm, showing between his heavy coat and the edge of his gloves. In the streetlight Jenny thought she saw a strange mark on it, but before she could register what it was, she jerked her head forward and clamped down hard with her teeth.

She tasted dirt and leather, from the glove, and

then blood in her mouth—from his wrist? His hand? A loud cry ripped the air. The other hand fell away from her throat, and she let out her own terrified scream. Then she was being thrown backward as the dark shape ran off.

Jenny rolled over, coughing. She still felt his fingers gripping her throat. She tried to close her ripped shirt, but she was shaking so badly she couldn't fix anything. She couldn't even sit up. She crawled to her jacket and bag, collapsed on top of them, and started weeping.

# CHAPTER 8

"Thanks for meeting me so early," Gail said as she leaned against the counter at Java Joe's.

Groggily, Jake rubbed his eyes and combed his fingers through his tangle of brown hair. "Nine o'clock on a Saturday morning is kind of early, especially after partying all night at the Club Z opening," he said. "Speaking of Club Z, it's a great place. We should do a story about it. You never made it over there last night, huh?"

Gail threw him a sidelong glance. "Are you kidding?"

"Oh, right. You told me on the phone about running into Liana Schmidt. I guess that didn't exactly put you in a party mood."

Gail sipped at her coffee. "That's not the least of it. Let's head over to the paper. Something else happened I want to tell you about."

Outside, the quad was deserted. Jake felt as though the Club Z party had ended five minutes ago. He and Nancy were two of the last people to leave, and he could still picture them laughing and dancing. The attraction between them had been hot, and she'd really loved the necklace.

"The DA called me again this morning," Gail began, snapping Jake out of his reverie, "to personally give me the wonderful news that someone was attacked and robbed, sometime after eleven o'clock last night."

"*Another* attack? Who was it?"

"Jenny Osborne."

Jake stopped in his tracks. "Jenny!"

Gail nodded and raised her eyebrows. "I didn't realize you knew her. Anyway, she's still in the University Health Clinic getting checked out. She was knocked around and has bruises on her throat, where the guy grabbed her. It sounded like he was trying to attack her sexually, but she bit him and he ran away. Luckily she's going to be all right."

Jake shook his head. "I can't believe it. Jenny hangs out in Nancy's suite all the time. Wow, when it happens to someone you know—"

"It's definitely getting closer to home."

"Was it Evanson?" Jake asked.

Gail shrugged. "That's what the DA believes. He asked me to think again about giving up my source."

"That's a low blow," Jake said irritably.

Gail didn't seem as angry. "I have to admit," she confessed, "I'm starting to have my doubts. I'm not sure I'll be able to live with Evanson getting away with robbery and assault when I could have done something to put him in prison. Maybe I *should* give up my source's name."

"But you guaranteed your source's secrecy," Jake fired back. "Steve says that breaking that oath is the worst thing a journalist can do. And I agree with him."

"Even after Jenny's attack?" Gail asked uncertainly.

Jake was thoughtful for a moment and then nodded. "Yes, as awful as Jenny's attack was, if Evanson's guilty, they'll get him. We need to see what Jenny has to say."

They were standing in front of the building that housed the *Wilder Times* office. Gail touched him on the arm.

"Thanks for the support," she said. "I hope you're right."

She led the way up the stairs to the newspaper office. But she froze on the top step and stood gaping at something. "Oh, no!" she cried.

"What?" Jake raced up the last few steps to the top.

But Gail didn't need to answer, because Jake saw it himself. The words were angrily scrawled in black spray paint over the walls: Gail Gardeski—Criminal Lover!

\* \* \*

Stephanie propped herself up against the bathroom sink, took one look at herself in the mirror, adjusted the straps of her dress, and moaned. Loudly. "You really did it this time."

Her eyes focused on the unfamiliar toothbrush, comb, and man's shaving equipment sitting on the countertop.

"How did I get here?" she asked herself. As if you don't know, a scornful voice in her head whispered back.

But clenching her eyes shut, she shook her head violently. "This *isn't* what I wanted!"

She stood and pictured the night before. Ten o'clock had passed, then ten-thirty, and still no Jonathan. He was supposed to be at the club by nine. The thought occurred to her that maybe he'd gotten into an accident, but the idea didn't stay long. Her sadness had quickly turned to disappointment, which transformed to rage.

Stephanie had been certain that Jonathan stood her up, and she decided to have fun anyway. All the old determination came back: forget Jonathan Baur—she wasn't going to waste the *entire* evening.

While she'd been thinking, Stephanie heard a familiar voice speak her name behind her. Tossing her thick, dark hair, she'd turned and had leaned back against the bar, flaunting her dress and everything in it.

"Why, look what the cat dragged in," she'd drawled when she saw who it was. "Glen."

Then she and Glen were out into the night, heading toward his blue sports car. He'd driven fast and furiously to his off-campus apartment house, where Stephanie had followed him up to his apartment and right into his bedroom.

Now Stephanie was clutching the edge of the sink. "Stop!" she demanded. But the images kept tumbling toward her. Glen kissing her neck. His hands running down the sides of her neck, reaching for the straps of her dress . . .

Stephanie's eyes flew open. She whirled. "I have to get out of here."

She stepped quietly back into the darkened bedroom. Glen was still an immobile lump under the tangled sheets and blankets on the bed. She picked up her jacket off the floor, slipped into her shoes, and headed for the door.

"Leaving so soon?" a voice crooned from the bed.

Stephanie didn't even turn around. "I'm not coming back here," she insisted.

"Just like you'd never kiss me again?"

"I mean it this time."

"Whatever you say, Stephanie," Glen replied. "Are you running off to your *boyfriend* now?"

A picture of Jonathan flashed before her eyes, and she felt a searing jolt, half pleasure and half pain. She couldn't wait to see him. But she was mad at him. She loved him. She hated him. He made her do this. How would he ever forgive her?

Without another word, Stephanie flung open

the door and bolted from Glen's apartment. Out on the street, it took her a few seconds to figure out where she was. Glen's apartment house was located in an unfamiliar part of town, and she was surrounded by strange houses and apartment buildings, and alien streets. She finally spotted Wilder's clock tower piercing the bright morning sky and headed in its direction.

He can't ever know, Stephanie thought to herself as she trudged toward campus.

She was going to see him at Berrigan's in— "Oh my gosh," she exclaimed as she looked at her watch. "In one hour!"

She quickened her pace to a slow trot.

I'm not worried, she tried to convince herself. I'm the master actress. He can't know—so he won't. It's that simple!

But as she crossed one strange street after another, reality came crashing around her. Lying to men when she needed to had always been easy before because she'd never cared about the men. But Jonathan was different. The simple fact was that she cared too much about him. So what was she doing?

Taking off her shoes, Stephanie sprinted through the lobby of Thayer Hall and headed for the stairs. "What's happening to me?" she asked herself.

"I just can't believe it!" Liz said angrily as she and Nancy hurried along the walk toward the

University Health Clinic. "I'm so mad that a woman was attacked again. And that it was Jenny! She wouldn't hurt a fly."

"I know. It makes me furious that none of us is safe walking around town or on campus," Nancy replied angrily, struggling to keep pace.

The phone call from Jake had come a half hour ago, waking Nancy from a deep, exhausted sleep. But the news about Jenny being attacked was like the shock from ice water, and when she knocked on Liz's door and told her what happened, they were dressed and on their way in minutes.

"It must have been that Cal Evanson, right?" Liz said as they bounded up the steps of the clinic.

Nancy shook her head. "Jake said the police know it couldn't be him."

Liz stopped dead in her tracks. *"Not* Cal Evanson?"

"Evidently, Jenny said she bit her attacker on the hand, and that he had a strange-looking mark on his arm, maybe on his wrist. Evanson doesn't have any bite wounds or any marks on his arm. And since he's under police surveillance, it would have been almost impossible for him to sneak out of his house and back in."

"Great," Liz groaned. "This is getting creepier and creepier. Now there are two attackers roaming around Weston."

Or maybe just one, Nancy thought to herself. And it's not Cal Evanson.

Upstairs, they found Jenny sitting up in bed in a hospital gown and neck brace.

"Hi, guys," Jenny said, stiffly moving her head. Liz took her hand. "Are you okay?"

"I will be. They said my neck'll be stiff for a while. Whoever it was has strong hands." Jenny gave a brave smile, but suddenly her eyes became moist. "Oh, you guys, I was so scared. It was horrible. He tore my necklace off, and then he started touching me. . . ." Jenny broke down crying as Liz and Nancy tried to comfort her.

"It's okay, Jenny," Liz said, her arms around Jenny. "You're safe now."

Jenny's tears finally subsided, and Nancy handed her another tissue. "I don't want to walk around this campus afraid," Jenny said, her voice choking with emotion.

Nancy sat on the edge of her bed. "They're going to catch this guy, whoever it is," she assured her.

"But it's not that Evanson guy," Jenny replied. "The detective in charge of the case told me. It's weird, though," she added, "the guy who jumped me looks so much like Cal Evanson. The same build, height, everything. But I definitely saw a mark on my attacker's wrist, like a tattoo. I guess Cal Evanson doesn't have one, so he's out of the picture."

"The police are thinking now it's a copycat crime," Nancy offered. "From what Jake said, the police are still sure that Cal Evanson is guilty of the other attacks."

"A copycat crime, huh?" Jenny shook her head.

Nancy and Liz exchanged looks. Nancy nodded. "That's the idea."

"Listen, Jenny, you need to get some rest," Liz said. "We'll come back later on, okay?"

Jenny gave Liz a list of clothes and things she needed from her dorm room, and Nancy and Liz left.

Out in the hall, Nancy's mind was racing. "I didn't want to say anything in front of Jenny and upset her," Nancy said to Liz, "but there is the possibility that Jenny's attacker is the same guy who committed the other crimes three years ago."

Liz looked surprised. "What do you mean? Nancy, what do you know?"

"Well, I've read the transcripts from the original trial and notes from Evanson's new lawyer. Oh, and I've been interviewing people connected with the case," Nancy said. "From what I've learned so far, Liz, I think Cal Evanson may not have committed the crimes he was accused of."

"What about the mark on the guy's wrist that Jenny saw? Did the stuff you read from the original trial say anything about the other women seeing a tattoo or something on the wrist of their attacker?" Liz asked.

Nancy shook her head. "No. But we don't

know exactly what Jenny saw. The mark on her attacker's wrist might have been dirt. Or maybe the other women didn't see it because it was hidden. It could have been anything."

"So you really think Cal Evanson is innocent," Liz said.

"More and more," Nancy said. "I have to get back to the dorm."

"I'm going over to Jenny's dorm to get the things she wanted," Liz said. "See you later."

Nancy hurried back to Thayer Hall. The campus was stirring to life. In the distance, she could hear the Wilder marching band practicing for the football game at Holliston Stadium.

She thought about what she had to do: finish a paper for a class and work up the article on Trisha Evanson to keep Gail happy. And she wanted to talk to Jake and tell him what a great time she'd had last night.

But when she reached the lobby, all of that vanished. Standing by the elevators was Trisha Evanson.

"Nancy!" she called out. "Did you hear about the attack last night?"

Nancy cringed when Trisha sounded almost happy about it. "I knew the victim," Nancy said flatly.

Trisha tried to apologize. "I'm sorry," she said. "Will she be okay?"

Nancy nodded, but she was a little annoyed at Trisha's obvious excitement.

"I just talked to Cal, and he told me he's been cleared of this attack. Doesn't that help prove that he's innocent of the other attacks, too?"

Nancy's heart went out to her. It was obvious she loved her brother, and that she'd do anything for him. And *think* anything for him.

"Look," Nancy said, "there's a theory going around about a copycat attacker," she explained, "meaning—"

Trisha scowled. "I know what it means. That this guy was just imitating Cal. But can't you understand that Cal's innocent?"

Nancy nodded. "Yes, I can see that as a possibility. But possibilities aren't good enough. Not when women aren't safe to walk around campus. We need proof."

Trisha narrowed her eyes. "You know the most ironic thing about all this, the thing that no one is willing to consider? He had no reason to attack or rob anybody. He always got along great with women. When he and I were growing up, he treated me like gold. We were great friends. Cal has dated lots of women and has been in a lot of healthy relationships. He's not just some psycho out to hurt women."

"I hate to tell you this, Trisha," Nancy said, "but other women tell a different story about Cal."

Trisha eyed her suspiciously. "Like who?"

"I talked to someone yesterday who wasn't surprised to hear that Cal might have been attacking women. He was a huge flirt, she said, and he gave off unpleasant vibes around women. She seemed pretty convinced."

"Really, and who was that?" Trisha demanded.

Nancy was about to say, when she swallowed her reply. "I don't think it's a good idea for you to get involved," she warned.

"Well, she couldn't really know my brother," Trisha insisted. "Why don't you talk to someone who does, an ex-girlfriend of his or something?"

"Any ideas?"

Trisha nodded. "Joan Rostenkowski. She's a waitress at the Purity Coffee Shop. Cal used to hang out there a lot. He and Joan dated for a while. It was kind of a messy breakup, but she wouldn't lie about him. She knows what kind of guy my brother is."

Nancy's mind was racing: Joan . . . Purity Coffee Shop . . . They used to date?

"Just something different about him," Joan had told her yesterday.

There *is* something different about Cal Evanson, Nancy realized. He was Joan Rostenkowski's ex-boyfriend!

# CHAPTER 9

*Dear Blondie: So it's a date! Tomorrow at 2 P.M. in Java Joe's. Our Deadhead T-shirts will find each other. Until then . . . Flash. P.S. Thanks for saying yes.*

"You're welcome," Holly murmured as she read the end of Flash's E-mail message, excitement building in her.

The quick knock on her door startled her, and a second later Soozie came waltzing in.

*"Please,"* Holly said as Soozie plopped down on Holly's bed, "come in."

"We have to talk about the weekly meeting," Soozie reminded her.

"I'll be downstairs in a few minutes," Holly said, going to her closet as Soozie wandered over to her computer.

"Is that the computer cuckoo you write to?" Soozie asked, checking out Holly's screen.

"Yup," Holly replied.

"You *are* going on a date with him!" Soozie cried. "I'm disappointed."

Holly just shrugged. She had learned a long time ago not to take Soozie or her catty comments seriously. Holly wanted to believe that somehow, somewhere, underneath her icy smooth permafrost exterior, Soozie was a normal person like everyone else. Maybe even a little more insecure. At least that's what one of Holly's psych major friends had advised her.

"Sorry to disappoint you, Soozie," Holly replied. "From what I know so far, he's a sweet guy. And we have a lot in common."

"Like not knowing what the other one looks like," Soozie quipped.

"We described ourselves," Holly said. "He sounds really cute."

"Did he come out and say that?" Soozie asked. "Hi, I'm Flash," she mocked. "And I'm really cute—except that this is the only way I can get a date, by talking to girls who can't see me."

"Ha, ha," Holly said, annoyed. "No, he wasn't quite that subtle."

"Well, how do you know he's telling the truth?" Soozie asked.

"If he's lying I'm going to find out in twenty-four hours," Holly said, exasperated. "So what would be the point?"

"What if he's a total dog?" Soozie asked, wrinkling her nose. "Then you're going to be stuck with him, and everyone will see! Why didn't you pick a less crowded place?"

"Because then you'd be saying, 'What if he's a nut case, then you're going to be stuck with him in a deserted place. Couldn't you pick somewhere more crowded?'" Holly replied, imitating Soozie's high-pitched voice perfectly.

Soozie threw up her hands. "Well, it's your social life." She peered again at the computer screen.

"How sweet," Soozie cooed. "You'll be in matching shirts."

"We're both Grateful Dead fans," Holly replied, "so we're wearing Deadhead T-shirts." Holly decided she was sick of Soozie and her annoying comments.

"Okay," she said, waving Soozie away. "I've been duly reminded of my duties as a house council member. You can leave now."

"Sometimes I still don't understand how you got voted vice-president," Soozie muttered, shrugging her shoulders as she opened Holly's door. "Meet me downstairs when you've finished romancing with Flicker, or Sparkle, or whatever his name is. All I have to say is that I think the whole thing's weird."

Holly breathed a sigh of relief as soon as Soozie was gone. Whatever reservations Holly had still harbored about meeting Flash evaporated.

If Soozie thinks it's a weird idea, Holly mused, then it's probably a great idea.

Holly looked back at her computer and grinned. So the showdown is set for tomorrow, she thought. Main event: Flash meets Blondie.

Holly could hardly wait.


"Hey, pick it up, sleeping beauty." The manager of the cosmetics department at Berrigan's snapped her fingers in front of Stephanie's eyes. "You have three customers waiting over at the counter. And you'll miss sales if you don't get a move on."

This day has been a nightmare! Stephanie thought to herself. It's been one customer after another since the store opened. I haven't had a chance to talk to Jonathan.

Which wouldn't have been a terrible thing, she knew, except that she kept rehearsing her lie about last night over and over in her brain and wanted to get it over with.

Stephanie walked slowly toward her cosmetics counter. She cringed when she realized she recognized the three customers. They were Wilder freshmen. Stephanie was still embarrassed about having to take a job to earn extra money now that her dad had cut off her credit cards.

"Stephanie? Stephanie Keats?" The high-pitched voice wavered between laughter and disbelief. "What are you doing working *here?*"

Stephanie stared back, amazed at how well she

was keeping her temper. "Earning money," she answered evenly. "That's why most people work." Gritting her teeth, she summoned her most pleasant and professional smile and asked, "Now, what can I get you ladies today?" She exacted her revenge by selling the three women twice as much makeup as they wanted to buy.

An hour later the floor was quiet, the cosmetics department was clear of customers, and Stephanie's feet were killing her. Slipping off her heels, she lowered herself onto a low stool behind the counter, resting her chin on her hands, and closed her eyes. Though it felt like hours, she'd napped only a minute or two when she heard her name calling her back.

"There you are!" Jonathan's deep voice rang out.

Stephanie's eyes snapped open, and she hopped to her feet. One look across the counter at Jonathan sent a wave of guilt and sadness crashing over her. He looked gorgeous in brown tweed pants with a linen shirt and an olive wool vest. Stephanie loved well-dressed men.

But there was no time to stop and smell the flowers. Her plan called for her to turn the tables on him before he knew what was coming.

"So glad you made time to show up last night," Stephanie said coolly.

"I'm really sorry," Jonathan said imploringly. "You won't believe it—"

Stephanie crossed her arms. "Won't I?"

"The manager's meeting here went from five to nine," Jonathan continued. "Afterward, I was totally fried. My feet hurt so badly from being on the floor all day, there was no way I could go dancing."

Stephanie's eyes glittered as she teased him. "You old man" was all she said.

Jonathan shrugged in agreement. "I've already done the college party scene," he explained calmly. "It's fun, but it's not such a big deal for me anymore." Obviously, he noticed Stephanie's disappointment. "Hey," he added quickly. "I still like to have fun. But the only thing I was good for after that meeting was stretching out on my bed."

Under the counter, Stephanie was wringing her fingers, but above it she was smiling mischievously. "Sounds good to me."

Jonathan cocked his head. "Did you have a good time at the club?"

"It would have been better with you. I waited all night."

Jonathan reached across the counter. "Steph, I did call the club, but it was so loud the bartender couldn't understand a word I was saying. I'm so sorry. Tell me you had a good time anyway. You danced with your friends all night?"

Stephanie hesitated, then nodded her head once, quickly. "All night," she said softly.

"Good." Jonathan smiled. "Then let's spend

tonight together. I'll take you out to dinner. We'll go to Marcel's—"

"It's so expensive!" Stephanie protested.

"It's the least I can do," he said, "for making you wait all night. I'm really sorry I missed the party now. It must have been an outrageous time."

Stephanie felt a sharp stab of guilt as a glimmer of Glen streaked across her eyes. But she quickly blinked him away.

Her plan was working. She shouldn't rock the boat. Unfortunately, the better her plan worked, the worse she felt. Jonathan was practically falling all over himself to apologize.

Stephanie knew that she should be the one doing the apologizing.


Ray was still feeling depressed as he paid for his burger at the front counter. He was on his way to meet Cory and Austin to start auditioning new members for the band, but he already had the feeling that the whole day would be a wash. And Ray knew exactly when this bad premonition had hit him—last night after talking to Karin at Club Z.

When Ray had introduced himself again, Karin had seemed a lot nicer than she had the first time they met.

"Is this your new band?" he'd asked.

"Not really," Karin had replied with a toss of her shoulder. "We just sort of threw ourselves together for this gig. But we're not committed to anything."

Ray had then broached the idea about Karin possibly joining up with him and the new band. "With your voice, I think we'd be great."

"You mean you, Cory, Austin, and *me?*" Karin had started laughing. "Are you kidding? I'm totally uninterested in playing with my ex-boyfriend, thank you very much.

Before Ray could say anything else, Karin had been back onstage, and Ray had to listen to another hour of her voice—a voice he wanted in his new band.

Ray knew he had to clear his mind to be able to listen to the people who were coming to audition. Maybe they'd find someone else as good for Radical Moves. But Ray knew he was just trying to make himself feel better. He took his change from the cashier and turned to the door.

And saw Karin on her way in.

When she looked up and noticed him, she faltered and then smiled. Ray walked over to her.

"Ray, right?" Karin asked. "Look, I'm sorry," she went on. "I heard your stuff with the Beat Poets on the radio and I think you're good. But there's no way Austin and I can be in a band together again," she added. "No way."

"Wait," Ray said, digging in the pocket of his jacket. "Before you say no, just listen to this."

He pressed a cassette into her hand. It was a

copy of the new Radical Moves demo he'd given to Montana.

"We're auditioning new members today and tomorrow," Ray said quickly, holding up his hand before Karin could reply. "And by the way, our name is Radical Moves."

"That's cool," Karin admitted after a pause. She stood looking down at the tape in her palm.

"Just listen to it," Ray urged again, and then turned and left the diner. Outside he pulled his jacket around him. Maybe the day hadn't been a total wash. There was still a chance that Karin would change her mind.

"No luck, huh?" It was late Saturday afternoon, and Kara was sitting at her desk, a textbook propped against a pyramid of soda cans in front of her.

Nancy returned the phone to the cradle and stared at it. "I've never heard anyone use the term, 'No comment,' ten times in under a minute before," she said good-naturedly.

"Lawyers are good at that," Kara quipped.

Nancy knew getting Cal Evanson to talk to her would be a long shot, but she figured she had to try anyway. Unfortunately Cal's new lawyer did know his stuff, and he wasn't letting Cal say a word to anyone until the trial.

Nancy stood up.

"Where to now?" Kara asked.

"I think I'll grab a cup of coffee—at the Purity Coffee Shop."

Driving downtown toward the Purity, Nancy's mind traveled through her last conversation with Joan, and it made her mad. Not saying anything about being Cal Evanson's ex-girlfriend was practically a lie, and you lie if you have something to hide. "But what could she be hiding?" Nancy wondered aloud.

As she pulled her car into the coffee shop parking lot, Joan was heading for her car, an old beat-up van.

"Hey, Joan," Nancy called, hopping out.

Joan lifted her head, her expression anything but happy. Without replying, she unlocked the door to her van and stepped in.

"There's something else I wanted to ask you," Nancy said, talking to her through the open window.

"I told you everything I know," Joan said curtly.

"I don't think so," Nancy said. "For instance, you conveniently left out the part about Cal Evanson being your ex-boyfriend."

Joan, who had been about to start the ignition to her car, leaned back against the seat and exhaled. "Who told you that?"

"Are you denying it?"

Joan shrugged. "What's the point? But I want it on the record that I didn't tell you only because I didn't want to get involved."

"Though by lying," Nancy interrupted, "you *do* involve yourself."

Joan sighed. "Look, the reason I didn't say anything is that when I broke off our relationship, Cal got really mad. He tossed some stuff around his apartment and hit a wall." Joan was obviously about to continue but stopped herself and said something else. "Let me put it this way: After watching him go berserk that night, I wasn't surprised to hear that he'd been arrested."

Nancy waited a beat. Something was missing, something crucial. What had Joan been going to say? She was still holding back, Nancy could tell. She was clutching the steering wheel and squeezing it. And she wouldn't look Nancy in the eye. She was definitely nervous.

"You're sure he never hit you or harassed you?" Nancy probed.

Joan looked away. She shook her head. But Nancy kept quiet. If there was anything she'd learned from journalism class and her work on the paper, it was to let the subject bring up the important questions by herself. The subject knows what she needs to tell—and usually *wants* to tell it.

Joan wasn't any different.

"I haven't told the police this," she began softly, "but I was attacked and robbed, too, when those other women were."

Nancy's jaw dropped. "You? By whom?"

"The same guy in the ski mask and gloves who

beat up the others. It *was* Cal. I could tell. And I should know, since we were together for a while."

Nancy shook her head in amazement. "But why *didn't* you tell the police?"

"Because," Joan said, "by the time the attacks started, I'd gotten engaged to someone, and he was the real jealous type—still is. I figured that since Cal and I had had a relationship before, my fiancé wouldn't believe I was a victim. He would have thought that Cal and I had been together or something, and Cal had beat me up." Joan rubbed her forehead, and Nancy noticed the tension on her face.

"And it's too late to tell the police about my attack," Joan said. "My fiancé is now my husband, and he would definitely think something was funny because I never told anybody three years ago."

Joan lifted her face to Nancy's, her eyes pleading. "Which is why *you* have to keep quiet about it, too," she implored. "I've already told too many people about this."

Nancy thought a moment. A small suspicion crept into her head. "Who *have* you told?" she asked.

But Joan's face was set in a determined expression. "Never mind. I've said too much."

"You know," Nancy said tentatively, "the editor-in-chief of the paper I work for has been doing a story on this, too. Her name is Gail Gardeski, and she knows I'm down here. We talked about it."

"You did?" Joan asked innocently, but her nervous eyes betrayed her.

Nancy swallowed. So she was right! Joan Rostenkowski was Gail's secret source. "Yes," she said.

Joan seemed to breathe easier. "Then Gail knows everything?"

Stunned, Nancy nodded.

"When Gail found out I was once Cal's girlfriend," Joan explained, "she promised me she'd print everything I said and not tell a soul my name. She said she'd help get that creep convicted again and keep me out of trouble."

"And you're absolutely positive it's Cal Evanson who's guilty of these attacks?"

Joan nodded convulsively. "Yes. Tell Gail thank you for keeping me out of the papers. I know she's getting in hot water over it."

Her mind racing, Nancy watched in flabbergasted silence as Joan drove off. Now she was positive Gail should give Joan's name to the DA. Whether Cal Evanson was guilty or innocent, Joan's testimony was a very important piece of evidence.

Noticing the time, Nancy quickly headed for a phone booth next to the coffee shop and dialed Jake's number. She was supposed to pick him up in fifteen minutes so they could get some dinner before the big Zeta bash, but she knew she was going to be late.

"I need another half an hour," she told him.

"No problem," he replied easily. "I'm just hanging out. Where are you?"

Nancy was about to blurt out her news but swallowed it instead. She and Jake never had secrets about their work; they even helped each other develop their stories.

But this is different, Nancy thought to herself. Jake already disagrees with me about my piece. So why pick a fight? Things last night were too good.

So she settled for a hint instead. "I've been working," she began.

"On—" Jake said, obviously curious.

Nancy flinched. She should have known Jake would have snapped at the bait. "Forget it," she said quickly.

Jake moaned. "Nance! You *know* you want to tell me. You tell me everything!"

She laughed. "I don't know why."

"Because you trust me."

Too true, Nancy agreed. Maybe he's changed his mind. Maybe he'd think this news is as huge as I do. "All I can say is that I've uncovered something big."

The line went dead with cool silence. "You're not digging into the Evanson thing, are you?"

"What if I am?"

Jake cleared his throat. "Because you

shouldn't. Gail specifically said to lay off the hard-hitting part of this thing. That's her story and she's on it. You have the sad sister angle."

"But you don't know what I know," Nancy insisted.

"It doesn't matter. You had orders—"

"Orders!" Nancy exploded into the phone. "What am I, a soldier? And you're not my father!"

For a few long seconds neither of them said a word. Nancy could hear Jake breathing hard.

"I don't know what I am to you anymore," she heard him mutter under his breath.

I don't believe it! she thought. I don't like this Jake Collins. I like the other one, the one who takes romantic trips with me in my car; the one who gave me the necklace last night; the sometimes goofy but always loving one who dances so crazily. Not this self-centered know-it-all.

"I'm not sure I like this," Nancy said, seething.

"Well, I don't either."

"You wouldn't have talked to me like this a month ago," Nancy said. "I don't know what's happened to us."

"Me neither," Jake shot back.

Nancy sighed.

"What was that?" Jake challenged her.

"That," Nancy said, "was the sound of my appetite leaving my body."

"Good!" Jake shouted. "Because I'm not hungry either."

"You know, it's amazing," Nancy said, "this is exactly how you acted when we were talking about me and my dad and Avery. You want me to have my own thoughts, Jake, as long as they agree with yours! This argument isn't about the Evanson case, is it? It's about me and you. It's about *everything!*"

"Hmm, fascinating theory," Jake said sarcastically. "You know, I'm suddenly kind of tired. As a matter of fact, I don't think I'm interested in that Zeta party after all."

Nancy was blind with anger. "Good, then I won't have to see you there!" she cried, and slammed down the phone.

# CHAPTER 10

All this talk about Natural Shades—all I see are babes, babes, babes!" a guy moaned.

"All *I* see is you," Jamal whispered to Pam.

Pam looked up at her boyfriend and smiled. They were at the Saturday night party Jesse had organized for the Natural Shades company and the would-be models. Loud music was blasting through the main hall in the African-American Cultural Alliance Center, and Pam and Jamal were surrounded by most of Wilder's African-American community.

"Tomorrow we'll find out which one of our Wilder women will be flaunting her face across the country," someone nearby was saying.

"Tomorrow seems like forever," Pam said, shivering nervously.

"I've got my money on you." Jamal grinned.

Pam blushed hotly as she watched Jamal's eyes travel up and down her body. She knew Jamal hadn't been happy about her entering the contest in the first place. But since she'd made it to the final round he'd been totally supportive.

Dancing in Jamal's arms, Pam stood on her toes and started nuzzling his neck. Then, suddenly, she felt him stiffen.

"What's wrong?"

He jabbed his thumb over her shoulder. "It's not you. That cosmetics jerk is here."

Pam turned to see Jesse Potter snaking his way through the crowd. He was grinning widely, and when he came a little closer to them, Pam could see why.

He had his arm wrapped lazily across someone's shoulder. That someone was Tamara, another of the Wilder students being considered for the Natural Shades modeling spot, which wasn't much of a surprise. Tamara was small and slender and very exotic looking, with her green eyes and coffee-colored skin.

He dropped so many hints about *me* being the winner, Pam thought to herself, confused. But now, seeing Jesse and Tamara together, I'm not so sure.

Jamal put his arm protectively around Pam and led her off the dance floor.

"I'd really like to punch that slimy jerk," Jamal muttered, stealing glances at Jesse and gritting his teeth. "He should be fired for what he did to you."

After her incident with Jesse at Java Joe's, Pam had gone back to her room and called Jamal. She'd told him about what had happened. Talking it out had made her feel less ashamed about the incident.

"Guys like him are always getting away with that kind of thing," Jamal continued. "It stinks."

"You were right about him," Pam admitted.

"Hey, man," Jamal said, tapping Dennis Larkin on the shoulder as he passed. "What happened with you two?" He nodded toward Tamara. Dennis was one of Jake Collins's roommates, and Pam knew he and Tamara had been dating off and on.

"He called her and asked her out," Dennis explained. "What can I say? The guy's got more clout than I do."

"That's cold," Jamal replied.

"Don't blame Tamara," Pam said. "I jumped at the chance to have coffee with him."

"I guess I'd have to get used to it anyway," Dennis said before moving on. "If she wins the contest, I'll hardly see her at all."

"You think she's going to win?" Pam asked Jamal softly.

"If I were the judge I know she wouldn't," Jamal replied, stroking Pam's neck.

"After all those hints Jesse made . . ." Pam paused. "I guess I'm silly to believe him."

"Pam," Jamal reminded her, "you entered the contest because it would be fun. And look how far you got. You're gorgeous and sexy and beautiful enough to model for anyone if you wanted."

Pam gave Jamal a kiss on the cheek. "You say all the right things. And you're right. I shouldn't take the whole thing so seriously. I mean, if I won, wouldn't I have to quit school or something? And that would be crazy! But I'm not going to let that bother me," she decided, watching Jesse and Tamara together. "I don't want to let *him* bother me, either. Don't worry, Jamal," she added, turning to him, "I'm just going to say hello."

Pam made her way through the crowd to Jesse. She didn't want there to be any hard feelings between them, in case Jesse's hints about her winning had been true and they'd be working together soon. It would be better and more professional not to make a big deal of it.

"Hey, Jesse"—Pam smiled—"congratulations. This party is a total hit."

Jesse turned to her, his face a complete blank. Then he turned back to Tamara.

"How about a dance, beautiful?" he whispered silkily, steering her past Pam.

Pam knew she was standing there with her mouth open, but she was too shocked to close it.

"What a total jerk!" she said when she finally got her wits together. He was even worse than Pam had imagined.

With so much on the line, she reasoned, the Natural Shades company wouldn't have left things to the last minute. The winner of the contest had to have been chosen weeks ago. And if Pam *was* the winner, there was no way Jesse Potter could get the Natural Shades company executives to change their minds just because Pam wouldn't sleep with him, she thought.

Was there?

"I don't think I'm ready," Bess said, taking a step back as she approached the porch of the Zeta fraternity.

The huge old house loomed in front of her—all the windows blazing with light. Pounding music seeped through the walls and Bess could feel the bass and drums rise through her feet. She turned to the group behind her. "Maybe you guys should go in without me."

All six of them—George, Will, Holly, Casey, Brian, and his friend, Chris Vogel—stepped forward and circled around her.

George put an arm around Bess's shoulders. "We'll do whatever you want to do."

"Brian and I put you through a mammoth rehearsal session today," Casey added. "If you're tired, we can just go back to Kappa and hang out."

"You know fraternity parties aren't my thing," Brian joked. "I'm only here because you twisted my arm."

Bess sighed. "You guys are so great. And now I feel totally pathetic."

"Bess," George said, "if you can't go in, then don't. It's not a test."

"I don't know," Bess replied, taking a deep breath. "Maybe it is sort of. I'm not sure I can go in, but I'm pretty sure I should. Hey, where's Nancy?"

George shrugged. "She called and said something about showing up later—and alone. I think she and Jake got in another fight. She said she really wanted to party."

"Then let's party," Bess said, not very enthusiastically.

She grasped the heavy iron door handle of the old frat house and pushed. They were engulfed with noise and warmth. Bess pulled herself together and moved forward into the crowded room.

Immediately, Bess found herself surrounded by Paul's frat brothers, being hugged from every side.

"Glad you made it!" one of them said.

"Wouldn't have been the same without you, Bess," another added.

"Bess!" Eileen cried, racing over with Emmet close behind her.

Bess allowed herself to be swept along by the enthusiasm and excitement. The whole place was alive with happy students celebrating the weekend. The music was fantastic, and of course, as always at Zeta parties, the dance floor was packed.

Everywhere she looked Bess was reminded of Paul. But she knew that if she started thinking about him, she wouldn't be able to stay. Luckily, there was an abundance of things to gossip about.

"So what's the latest from your cyber-hunk?" Bess asked Holly.

"Who's this hunk?" George asked.

"Holly's having an on-line love affair," Bess explained. "It's very romantic—they *type* to each other."

"I don't know why everyone seems to find this so bizarre," Holly scoffed. "It's just like writing letters."

"So," Bess teased. "any new *flashes* of inspiration lately?"

"Well, if you mean the date we made to meet each other," Holly said, her eyes sparkling, "then yes! Java Joe's at one tomorrow. And speaking of my big date, I was wondering if you wouldn't mind coming, too."

"On your first date?" Bess asked.

"Not to sit with me." Holly laughed. "Just to go to Java Joe's, and be there—in case I need you. You know, in case he turns out to be dorky or a weirdo."

Bess could see that Holly was excited, but also nervous and worried. It had to be strange to meet someone for the first time, someone to whom you'd been writing for weeks.

"Of course," Bess assured her. "What about it, George?" she asked, turning to her cousin. "Meet me for coffee at one o'clock?"

"And get to see the first date?" George laughed. "You bet. It sounds like fun."

Holly squeezed Bess's fingers. "I hope so," she murmured.

"Since you made it through the front door, you must be ready to dance," Brian said, coming over to Bess and taking her hand.

Bess laughed at Brian's goofy enthusiasm, but she wasn't sure she was ready to go along with it. She was about to pass when, to her surprise, she realized she did want to dance.

This time, thinking about Holly and her mystery man wasn't depressing, it was exciting. Exciting to think about someone falling in love and to remember that feeling. Nancy was right—this Zeta party was the best place for Bess to have a good time.

"I'd love to," Bess said, recalling all the good times she had had with Paul. "I always love to dance here."

Gail could hear the huge Zeta party outside. Someone was checking the sound system. People were crisscrossing the quad, laughing into the night.

Laughter. When was the last time *you* laughed? Gail thought to herself.

Sitting in her office at the *Wilder Times,* her

feet on her desk and hands behind her head, Gail scanned the note cards she'd pinned to the opposite wall. On each card was written a piece of the Cal Evanson puzzle—testimony or evidence. By spreading things out she could shift things around until they made enough sense for her to write a story.

Right then Gail was staring hard at the card marked 'Witness X.' Though she knew she was a student, she felt light-years away from Wilder University. The Cal Evanson case had brought real life crashing into her insulated college life: the district attorney, secret testimony, court orders, jail . . .

"Tell me what to do," she said out loud to herself.

"Don't give in."

The voice came from the darkened outer office of the newspaper. As she kicked her feet to the floor, Jake stepped into the light.

"How long have you been standing there?" she demanded.

"I just got here," Jake replied. "What are you doing here? It's Saturday night, in case you didn't know."

Gail sunk deeper into her chair. "Work is the only thing that keeps me sane these days."

Jake nodded forlornly. "I know what you mean."

Gail noticed that Jake was dressed to party. "I

think the more interesting question is, what are *you* doing here?"

Jake leaned against the open door and thrust his hands into his pockets. "That's a long story. And not a happy one."

"Have a seat," Gail said. "The doctor is in."

Jake laughed. "The doctor needs distraction from her own problems?"

Gail poked at a pile of letters collapsed across her desk. "Look at these. Insults. Threats. Advice. I was trying to drown my problems in busywork, but I'm running out of it. So go ahead, tell me your problems."

Jake was staring at her strangely. "I can't tell you all of it," he said. "But let's just say Nancy and I aren't getting along."

"What, trouble in paradise?"

"Unfortunately," Jake muttered.

Gail tried to wave his worries away with, "You guys'll work it out."

Jake tilted his head. "That's just what everyone else says," he replied. "Except, of course, Nancy and me."

"Knock, knock—"

Gail looked up. "Steve? What are you doing here?"

Steve Shapiro breezed into the room. "I was working late and saw your lights on. I wanted to bring these by. I think they'll cheer you up."

Gail was already feeling better being around

friendly faces. She noticed the sheets of papers clutched in Steve's hand. "What are they?"

"They," Steve said, dropping them on her desk, "are faxes from almost every major journalist in the area. They're all behind you."

Gail picked her way through the pile. Phrases like "your primary obligation," "story first," and "proud of you" leaped out at her.

"Wow," she exhaled on a single breath.

"Do you believe me now?" Jake asked. "You can't give in."

Gail noticed that he seemed more determined than ever that she refuse to name her source. Which made her curious. His newfound problems with Nancy and the controversy over this case seemed to be connected.

But there were more important things to worry about. Suddenly she was less tired. The image of Liana Schmidt still burned in her memory. But this case seemed bigger than one person. Bigger, even, than one writer. Who was she to challenge a journalist's right to protect her sources?

A glint came to Steve's eye. "Feeling righteous again, are you?"

A slow grin tugged at the corners of Gail's mouth. "Oh, yes, I think I am."

"That was so delicious," Stephanie purred, holding tight to Jonathan's arm. "I'm really glad we decided to walk to my dorm. I need to burn off some of this food. I'm so stuffed!"

"Why don't we go back to my place," Jonathan suggested. "We'll light some candles. . . ."

Stephanie put a finger to his soft lips. "Let me just imagine the rest."

She circled him in her arms and lifted her mouth to his and lost herself in his embrace.

"Hey, you lovebirds!"

Stephanie fell back. Overcome by the romance of Jonathan's affectionate attention and sweet words, she'd lost track of where they were: frat row. The mansion-size houses were lined up on both sides of the street. And Zeta was raging, the crowd spilling out the front door.

"Over here!"

Stephanie squinted through the darkness until she spotted Casey, Eileen, and Emmet waving from the brick wall around Zeta's porch.

"I forgot all about that party," Stephanie muttered.

"Which is a good sign?" Jonathan wondered.

"Yes!" Stephanie replied. "I had been looking forward to it all week."

"Then let's head over," Jonathan offered agreeably. "We can go back to my place after."

But Stephanie froze. She stared past her friends into the massive number of party-goers. The truth was, she wouldn't have minded going in if it weren't for the fact that somewhere in that crowd might be a face she'd do anything to avoid.

Glen could be in there, she thought.

"No way," Stephanie insisted. She took his hand and began to tug on it. "Home. Now."

Jonathan shrugged and started to follow. But before they got very far, Casey, Eileen, and Emmet started shouting at them again. Then they started dancing.

Jonathan was watching the party-goers. "I missed the Club Z party, Steph," he said. "This'll be fun. I'd like a dance or two. Just a couple songs, then we'll go."

Jonathan wasn't taking no for an answer. Before Stephanie knew it, he was leading her through the crowd, up the steps, and into the dancing throng.

"This is great!" he cried, and started to dance.

"Yeah, great," Stephanie muttered under her breath. She'd never been around so many people and felt so alone.

Stephanie's sixth sense picked up on Glen before her eyes did. She twirled around, then quickly back again, turning her back to the door.

"Something wrong?" Jonathan yelled.

Stephanie flashed her best who-me? smile, then tried to peek over the crowd to see if the door to the kitchen was open. She remembered she'd escaped through there before, to get away from some guy, or maybe to leave with a different guy. She forgot. But she knew it led to the back door—and to safety.

"I'm kind of tired," Stephanie said, but Jonathan didn't hear her. He was too busy having a good time. Gritting her teeth, she continued to dance, watching Glen watch her—until she noticed Casey. She was against the big fireplace and had both Stephanie and Glen in her line of sight. Casey raised her eyebrows.

Rolling her eyes, Stephanie mouthed, "Help!"

But Casey just wagged her finger.

Unbelievably, the music slowed and quieted as a romantic tune seeped through the speakers. Dancers coupled up and started swaying slowly in the half dark. Jonathan's arms slid around Stephanie's waist. Almost overcome with anxiety and sadness about the night before, Stephanie buried her face in his shoulder so the rest of the world could vanish. Suddenly it was just the two of them.

This feels so nice, she thought to herself. How could I ever want anything else?

"Stephanie?"

Stephanie felt Jonathan stirring. Someone was calling her name, but it wasn't Jonathan.

"Who said that?" Jonathan asked, lifting his head.

Stephanie looked right and left in panic. She saw no way out—except one.

Taking Jonathan's face in her hands, she held him in the steamiest kiss they'd ever had. The harder Stephanie kissed him, the harder she wanted to.

"Let's get out of here," she said, and pulled Jonathan toward the back door.

"Where—" Jonathan said.

Stephanie pushed ahead through the crowd—toward the freedom and privacy of the night.

Outside, she led him quickly around the back of the house and toward the street. Though the party was safely behind her, she could feel, like a cold wind against her back, Glen's eyes, watching her go. And they were laughing.

"Let's go!" she cried. She quickened her pace from a walk to a slow run. "I have some very private—and very exclusive—plans for us!"

Nancy could only shake her head as she watched Stephanie and Jonathan hurry out the back door of the frat. "What a soap opera!"

"I couldn't agree more."

Drink in hand, Nancy turned and smiled. It was Terry Schneider, head of the Focus Film Society and the current bane of Jake's existence. Jake had always saved a special dose of resentment for Terry, who with his tall, muscular good looks was not only a dead ringer for Nancy's ex, Ned Nickerson, but was also interested in Nancy for himself—and hadn't made a secret of it.

Nancy couldn't deny that in black jeans and a black T-shirt, Terry was the picture of simple sophistication.

Abruptly Nancy heard Jake's words echoing from the night before: "I need you as much as anyone could need anybody."

"What a surprise to see you," Nancy said, casting around uneasily.

Laughing, Terry cocked his head. "Why? Half the university is here."

Nancy shrugged. "Sorry. I'm just in a weird mood, I guess."

"Why aren't you dancing? Where's Jake?"

Feeling a prick of paranoia, Nancy tossed a wary glance over her shoulder. No Jake. Instead of replying, she fixed Terry with a blank look.

Where *was* Jake? she wondered. Nancy had spent an hour at the party wandering from one group of friends to the other. She felt as if she were surrounded by a plastic bubble, in her own world.

She missed Jake, but she was determined to go to the party in spite of him. She was mad at him, and she wanted to have fun.

"Well, if you're dateless," Terry said, lifting the drink out of Nancy's hand and leaving it on a nearby table, "I hope you won't mind if I ask you to dance."

As Nancy lifted her eyes to Terry's face, George's warning from a couple days ago came back to her: "Just don't do anything that can't be undone."

Nancy looked at Terry. It's just one dance! she argued with herself.

She tossed her reddish blond hair over her shoulder, and hooked her arm through his. "I won't mind at all."

# CHAPTER 11

An early morning run was just what I needed, Pam thought to herself, enjoying the familiar burn in her thighs. She rubbed her legs and stretched happily.

This whole Natural Shades thing is turning into a Natural Nightmare! Pam said to herself. I'll be glad when it's over.

Not that she wasn't still nervous about the announcement. Not that she didn't still harbor a small hope that she'd win.

Unfortunately, the waiting and the tension were wearing on her. And last night's scene with Jesse had been a real bummer. It had given her a bad feeling about the whole thing.

Forget it, Pam thought. She still had a few hours to kill before the announcement in the afternoon. And what better way to keep her mind off modeling than shopping? But first, a hot cup of coffee and the crossword puzzle.

Pam was about to pop into the convenience store to buy the Sunday paper, when she saw a bright flash of red across the street. When she looked up, she realized she was near the College Motel. That was where Jesse Potter had said he was staying.

Pam's eyes traveled to the front door, where Jesse was just coming outside. Under his open jacket, Pam could see his bright red shirt untucked and rumpled. And, Pam realized with a gasp, he wasn't alone. There was a woman with him. While Pam watched they locked themselves in a steamy embrace, right on the sidewalk. Even before she turned around, Pam knew who it was.

They broke from their kiss, and Tamara, wearing the same clothes Pam had seen her in the night before, started down the street, a happy grin on her face.

I can't believe she spent the night with him, Pam seethed. Isn't that the kind of thing the Natural Shades company should know about?

Instantly, Pam imagined what it would look like. One girl accusing another of dirty tactics.

Pam didn't want everyone to think she was out to smear her competition—but it would be hard for the judges to think of it any other way.

I'll bet Jesse told her some of the same things he told me, she mused. Did he drop the same hints about working together, or not being anxious about the announcement? Did Jesse even know who the winner was for sure? Or could it be whoever he wanted it to be?

Pam gritted her teeth and kept walking. There was nothing she could do about it now. If Jesse had that much influence about who would be the winner of the contest, then . . .

Only a couple more hours to wait to find out, Pam thought sadly.

"It's good to see you here,' Jeanne Glasseburg said as Bess took her place on the stage. It was exactly eleven o'clock. "I just want to say again how sorry I am about the accident you were in. And about your boyfriend. It must be very hard."

"Thank you," Bess replied, feeling her throat close up and her eyes begin to tear.

Don't blow it, Bess quickly told herself. The last thing she wanted was to break down the way she had with Brian and Casey. This was Bess's only chance to get into this acting class, and she couldn't afford to blow it with a sobfest. Bess steeled herself and forced away her tears and thoughts of Paul.

"So tell me who your character is?" Ms. Glasseburg asked, looking up at Bess from the front row of the small theater.

This time there was no Brian to make her laugh, and no Casey to give her advice. Bess took a deep breath and stood on the stage front left, according to the stage directions.

"I'm doing a scene about a woman whose husband has deserted her," Bess replied.

"All right." Ms. Glasseburg nodded, making a note on her pad. "Whenever you're ready . . ."

Bess gave herself a moment to think about the scene and where her character had been before she entered, then took a calming breath and jumped in. She tried hard not to think about Paul as she plunged ahead.

"Um, I'm sorry. Bess, do you mind stopping for a minute?" Ms. Glasseburg asked after Bess had only gotten a few lines into it.

What have I done wrong? Bess wondered, feeling so embarrassed she wished she could just slink off the stage.

"Your reading is a bit flat," Ms. Glasseburg said, standing at the edge of the stage. "Basically, you're showing no emotion at all."

"Oh." Bess felt her face flare with the heat of embarrassment.

"I understand that the scene is very straightforward," Ms. Glasseburg continued. "But there should be a lot of barely controlled disappointment, hurt, and even anger in this character." Ms. Glasseburg shrugged. "I'm not hearing any of that."

"I'm sorry—" Bess started to say.

"Let me give you one piece of advice right now," Ms. Glasseburg interrupted. "It's essential for an actor to tap into her feelings, not push them away. If there's something painful going on in you and you're spending energy keeping those feelings down, you just won't have anything left to give to your character."

"I see," Bess muttered. "Thanks for the advice. I'm sorry I wasted your time."

"Bess?" Ms. Glasseburg asked, a stern expression on her face. "Where do you think you're going?"

Bess looked up, surprised. "I thought," she said, "I thought this meant my audition was over."

"But I haven't seen anything yet," Ms. Glasseburg said. She pulled a playbook from her bag and began flipping through it.

"Oh, yes." Ms. Glasseburg smiled as she found the right page. "I'd like you to try something else. Read through this speech." She showed Bess the long monologue.

"Without any preparation?"

"You can handle it," Ms. Glasseburg replied. "Though if you aren't willing to try—"

"No, no," Bess said quickly. "I'll do it."

"Just to set the scene, this young woman is talking to her best friend," Ms. Glasseburg explained. "She's confessing her love for the town doctor."

Bess nodded and walked to the center of the stage. She glanced quickly down the page to see if there were any stage directions she could use.

"And, Bess," Ms. Glasseburg called from the

front row of seats. "Remember, use your emotions. Don't hide from them."

" 'I've felt this way for so long,' " Bess began. " 'But he doesn't notice—' "

You're stiff! Bess realized. Relax, relax . . .

" 'Now he's gone, and I still hear his voice, and see him. I can't stop feeling how much I love him—' "

How much she loved Paul.

Tears came to her eyes, and she quickly wiped them away so she could keep reading.

" 'I think of him all the time. Oh, I'm crazy, aren't I—' "

She was hardly aware of when she'd lifted her arm, but Bess was holding it out toward the empty seats, beseeching the darkness. She *was* crazy, wasn't she? She had to be crazy to be living every day without Paul. It wasn't fair that she couldn't talk to him anymore, smile with him, touch him.

I can't ever tell him again how much I love him, Bess realized, her breathing unsteady as she stood on the silent stage, the playbook dangling by her side.

"Okay," Ms. Glasseburg said, coming to stand in front of her. She gave Bess a warm smile. "Thank you very much. I'll call you in a few days to let you know."

Bess just nodded.

At least she was smiling, Bess thought, as she

gathered up her stuff and ducked out the side door.

The smile would have made Bess really hopeful—if only she had an idea about how the audition went. She thought back to the scene she'd just read, but her mind was a blank.

She shook her head. She'd been so wrapped up in her memories of Paul that she didn't have a clue about how she'd performed.

Stephanie opened one eye, then the other. Then closed them both. Again.

Sitting at her desk, she shielded her face from the morning sunlight slanting in through the blinds and felt for her books. Theoretically, she was supposed to be studying.

That *is* why you called in sick to work, she reminded herself. To study. Then she checked in with her screaming headache: still there. I *am* sick, she thought.

Stephanie corrected herself. No, she'd called in sick because she'd managed to hide the truth from Jonathan during the dark of night but didn't think she could keep it from him in the light of day.

Jonathan had probed her about why they had to leave the party so quickly. Eventually, she'd managed to stop his interrogation with kisses. Though, deep inside, she knew that *he* knew she was keeping something from him.

An hour ago she'd left his apartment, leaving

a note saying she needed to pick up her clothes at her dorm. She'd see him at work.

"Or not," Stephanie muttered.

She lifted her head at the sound of knocking, not at her door but at the suite door in the lounge. "Somebody get that!" she cried.

But the knocking continued.

"Where *is* everybody?" she wondered aloud as she shoved herself back from her desk. "They're all probably having breakfast together downstairs," she said, sneering. "A nice little lovefest."

She stalked through the suite and swung the door open.

"Well, hello."

"You!" Stephanie cried at Glen standing in the doorway.

As usual, when she saw him, she was overcome by a lethal combination of disgust, guilt—and desire.

The fact was, as much as she would have liked him to, he just *couldn't* be an ugly sight. In fact, he was more handsome than she remembered, with a chiseled chin and strong, muscular arms.

Quickly Stephanie started to close the door. But Glen jammed his foot in the crack. "Wait a second," he said. "I won't bite. Promise."

Stephanie peered past him into the hallway. Not a soul in sight. She listened for signs of life in her suite. Thankfully, there wasn't a sound. "It's not you I'm worried about," she whispered.

"Good, then you'll let me in," Glen said presumptuously, and stepped into the lounge.

"Will you get out of here?" she demanded. She glared at him unconvincingly. "Can't you take a hint?"

Glen's eyes traveled slowly down Stephanie's lean body. Suddenly, she remembered that when she'd gotten home she'd changed out of her clothes and into a flimsy silk robe—with nothing on underneath.

Folding her arms over her chest, Stephanie fixed him with a steady glare. "I guess that means no." Sighing exasperatedly, she closed the door behind him. "If I can't get rid of you, you'd better get in here." Scowling, she led him into her room and slammed the door.

"After all, you don't want to give your suitemates the wrong impression." Glen laughed. "Where's your boyfriend?"

"What if I told you he'd be here in two minutes?"

"Then I'd say you're in trouble."

"Well, I'm not," Stephanie replied tightly. "He's at work. So what do you want?"

Glen stepped toward her. Not one to give in, Stephanie stood her ground. "Back off!"

Glen reached for her waist. "If you didn't want me here, you wouldn't have invited me in."

Stephanie pushed him away. Even if he was drop-dead gorgeous, he'd become a monumental pain. "You invited yourself. If you came over because you think I'm just going to fool around with you again, forget it. But if you want to talk—"

"Then let's just talk," Glen said quickly. He looked around the room as if he were trying to find something to talk about. "What'll it be?"

"Me."

"I like that."

"And Jonathan Baur."

The playful spark in Glen's eyes snuffed out. "So that's his name."

Stephanie nodded. "And you may find this hard to believe, but I'm really crazy about him. *Jonathan,* Glen. Not you."

"It didn't seem that way at Club Z."

Stephanie flinched at the thought of that night. "That," she said firmly, "was a mistake."

"Uh-huh," Glen replied dubiously.

"Well," she said, "I was just playing with you because I was bored. Jonathan's a man. He's out of your stratosphere."

Stephanie could tell she'd hurt him. His cockiness had wilted a little.

"I think I get the message," he finally said. "Sorry I bugged you."

Stephanie eyed him. She actually liked him this way, a little less sure of himself.

"It's not as though I find you unattractive," she added.

"If anything happens between you and Jonathan," he said, "you know who to call."

Stephanie's reply was cold and businesslike. "I'll keep it in mind."

She reached past him for the door. But just as she did, someone knocked on it. As she yanked it open, she found herself face-to-face with Jonathan, smiling sweetly, a single red rose clutched in his hand.

"I thought I'd come over during my break," Jonathan said.

"How—how'd you get in here?" Stephanie stammered.

Jonathan pointed back into the lounge. "The front door was left open. Why did you call in sick, Steph? You looked pretty healthy to—" His expression fell.

Stephanie hid her eyes. It didn't take a genius to know that Jonathan had spotted Glen, in her room, with her wearing nothing but a thin silk bathrobe.

Jonathan's face reddened, his nostrils flared.

Defeated, she waved her hand weakly. "This isn't what it looks like."

"Look, man, she's right," Glen said, holding up his hands. "Everything's cool. Nothing happened."

"Oh, I bet it didn't." Jonathan seethed. He dropped the rose on the floor. "I knew something was strange last night." He raised an angry finger at Glen. "That's the guy you were kissing on the sidewalk in front of Berrigan's the other day!

150

Was *he* there at the Zeta party last night, Stephanie?"

"You have to believe me, I love *you!*" Stephanie cried, and reached for his hand.

But Jonathan snatched it away. "I can't believe I ever trusted you. I'm such an idiot!"

Turning on his heels, he slammed out of the suite without looking back.

# CHAPTER 12

Nancy studied the Sunday morning brunch crowd filling the booths in the Purity Coffee Shop. Joan Rostenkowski and a second waitress were moving quickly between the tables, taking orders and bringing out plates heaped with pancakes and omelettes and hash browns. Nancy felt guilty for ordering just a cup of coffee. All the food *did* smell awesome, but she just couldn't bring herself to eat. She was racked with guilt and exhilaration—and fatigue.

The fact was, she and Terry had danced late into the night, and she'd had a great time. She was grateful for the distraction from her fight with Jake and from the Cal Evanson case. Afterward Terry had walked her home, talking about his plans to go to graduate school for filmmaking. But the air between them as they walked crackled with electric anticipation. She knew he liked her, but he'd been the perfect gentleman and had even said he hoped she and Jake worked things out.

It all felt so innocent but dangerous, and Nancy realized she'd liked the feeling!

Nancy turned her thoughts to Jake. They'd work things out, somehow. But as she cupped her hands around her mug of coffee and started thinking about their situation, the war started to wage all over again in her brain.

*I can't believe he still hasn't called to apologize. Then again, you haven't called him.*

"Can I get you anything else?"

Joan was standing by Nancy, her order pad ready. Nancy looked up at her and blinked, almost forgetting why she was here. The day before, when Joan let it slip that she was Gail's secret source, Nancy was so surprised she forgot to ask her a few crucial things, such as whether she'd noticed a dark mark on the wrist of her attacker.

"Yeah, a couple of quick answers," Nancy said.

Joan rolled her eyes, then gave her head a hard shake. "Too busy. Later."

She splashed fresh coffee into Nancy's mug and sauntered away. Nancy left some change on the table. She knew Joan wouldn't be free for a couple of hours.

Nancy's eyes settled on the phone booth outside—the same phone booth she'd called Jake from yesterday and fought with him.

Okay, I'll be the adult and make the call, she decided. She fished a quarter out of her pocket and got up to leave. Before she could, something made her sit back down. A large, bearish man wearing faded blue jeans under a black leather jacket pushed his way through the crowd at the front. It was Larry, the guy she'd bumped into on her way out of the diner on Thursday, the one Joan had greeted so affectionately. Only this time one of Larry's hands was swathed in a gauzy bandage.

It was the bandage that got Nancy's attention. She watched as he sidestepped to an empty stool and slipped off his leather jacket. But as his jacket came off, so did the bandage. Larry quickly rewound the gauze, but not before Nancy could see what was underneath: a very clear and very painful-looking bite mark!

Acting on a hunch, Nancy shifted in her seat for a better look. Larry ordered coffee and eggs and reached for the jar of sugar with his good hand. As he did so, his sleeve crept up his arm. And Nancy had to swallow a gasp. There, on his wrist, was a dark tattoo, the same tattoo Jenny had seen.

"It's Larry," Nancy said under her breath. "*He* attacked Jenny!"

\*     \*     \*

It was five minutes to one, and Holly was having her hundredth bout of second thoughts.

It had taken her more time to get ready this morning than it usually did for a date, even though she was wearing some of her most unspectacular clothes. She'd picked out her favorite Grateful Dead T-shirt and her most comfortable pair of jeans. She'd left her blond hair hanging loose and wavy around her shoulders. Was she really ready to meet Flash? When Holly saw the entrance to Java Joe's up ahead, she almost stopped in her tracks.

What am I thinking? she asked herself, suddenly feeling just like the pathetic computer geek Soozie had teased her about being.

"I'm not this desperate for a boyfriend, am I?" Holly wondered out loud. It's not as though I went on-line specifically to find a boyfriend. The chat groups were fun! It's natural when two people like Flash and me get along so well.

As if you even know how he "gets along" at anything, Holly mused. You don't even know yet if you like him. What if he can't talk to you in person?

Too late to back out now, Holly admonished herself. Flash is probably inside waiting. Maybe he's already seen me!

Taking a deep breath, she pulled open the door to Java Joe's and went in. The place was pretty full, which wasn't surprising, considering the chilly weather and that it was Sunday afternoon.

Most of the tables were buried under sections of the Sunday papers.

Holly quickly scanned the room as she unzipped her jacket. When she saw Bess and George at a table in the corner, she smiled in relief. Bess gave her a little wave and shrugged her shoulders as she glanced around. No guy in a Deadhead shirt yet.

Holly put her jacket at an empty table and went to the coffee bar to order a hot chocolate. She checked her watch: 1:07. When she paid for her hot chocolate, Holly realized her hands were shaking.

"Blondie?" Someone tapped her on the shoulder when she was back at her table. Holly almost jumped. She took a deep breath, then turned around.

"Flash?" she asked, looking up with astonishment.

The guy smiled, his eyes lighting up like lamps. "Please," he said, speaking with a French accent, "now I think you can call me Jean-Marc."

"And I'm Holly," she replied as she watched Jean-Marc settle himself at the table. He wasn't drop-dead gorgeous, Holly realized, but he was nice looking, with short black hair and high cheekbones—very European looking, she thought. And great eyes.

"You're French!" Holly exclaimed, surprised. She realized it sounded like an accusation and she blushed. "Sorry."

"It's okay," he replied. "I'm actually French-Canadian. So no big ocean between us," he teased. "And I'm here as an exchange student for the year."

"Only for the year," Holly repeated. Did that matter? she suddenly wondered.

Jean-Marc shrugged and stared down at the table.

Cautiously, Holly raised her eyes toward Bess and George. They both had on the same ear-to-ear grin, and were giving her a double thumbs-up.

"H-O-T!" Bess mouthed.

Holly sighed. This was a lot harder than typing into a computer screen.

"Great shirt," she finally said, nodding at his colorful tie-dye.

"Yours, too," Jean-Marc replied, clearing his throat. Then silence.

"I'm thinking of things to say," Holly finally blurted out. "But I'm having a hard time getting them out."

"I know," Jean-Marc agreed, glancing at her quickly. "It's very distracting to have someone to look at instead of my computer screen." He paused. "Especially someone so pretty."

"Thanks," Holly replied, feeling the blush rise to her cheeks. "There is one question I haven't asked you yet, though," she added.

"Only one?" Jean-Marc replied. "That's too bad. This will be a pretty short friendship, then."

Holly smiled. "It's about how we met," she

said. "You never did tell me why you started going on-line in the first place."

"After a few weeks here I wanted to find a new way to meet people. Sometimes, it takes a while to fit in," Jean-Mac admitted, with a sweet smile. "Being French-Canadian or speaking English with a French accent doesn't make me a more interesting person than anyone else, but most people can't seem to get past it."

"You don't like it here at Wilder?"

"Of course I do," Jean-Marc replied. "But it's hard to always have to be Jean-Marc the guy with the accent, or Jean-Marc the foreign guy. I'm not really that foreign. I wear the same clothes, I live in the same part of the world. Back home I'm a very regular person."

"I understand what you're saying," Holly replied. "But I don't agree."

"You don't?" Jean-Marc acted upset.

"I doubt, even at home, that you're just a regular person." Holly smiled. "Don't forget you've already told me some of your secrets."

"That's true," Jean-Marc answered.

Holly could see that he was actually reddening. Her heart started beating even faster.

"And I hope you don't mind," he continued. Shyly, he reached out and took one of her hands in his. "You know more about me than anyone else on campus," he said. "In fact, you know more about me than anyone else in this whole country!"

"You make it sound so unfair," Holly replied, staring at her hand in his. "But you know some of my best secrets, too."

"I like that," Jean-Marc said. "I hope that things between us won't change."

"You mean now that we've actually met each other?" Holly laughed. "I was thinking about that, too. I was worried."

"Worried?" Jean-Marc asked, catching Holly's eyes with his.

"That I might lose Flash," Holly admitted, her voice soft.

"Well, I think that's already happened," Jean-Marc said, his face serious.

"Why?" Holly asked, hurt. She pulled her hand away from his. "What's the matter!"

"Nothing," Jean-Marc replied, breaking into a smile. He reached out and lightly touched her fingers. "You've already lost Flash," he explained. "And I've lost Blondie. But we have found each other."

"Is he playing 'Chopsticks' again?" Cory asked in a loud whisper. "I swear it sounds like 'Chopsticks.'"

Ray knew it wasn't the famous beginner's piano exercise they were listening to, but it might as well have been. The keyboardist who was playing wasn't awful, just a three-chord wonder. Not exactly an inventive musician. And not the kind of person they needed for Radical Moves.

Just like every other person we've listened to the last two days, Ray realized, rubbing his hand over his face, disappointed and exhausted.

"Okay, okay," Austin finally interrupted the keyboardist. "That's great. Really great. I think we've heard enough, right, guys?" He looked back at Cory and Ray, who both nodded enthusiastically. "We'll call you in a few days and let you know."

As the keyboardist packed up and wrote down his number for them, Ray wondered what had happened with Karin. He'd kept hoping all day yesterday and even today that she'd show up. At this point it was pretty obvious she wasn't interested.

"I doubt she even listened to the tape," Ray muttered.

"Who?" Austin asked, overhearing him. "The hot blond radio babe?"

Ray hadn't actually told the other guys about speaking to Karin. He'd decided to cross that bridge when they came to it. Only now it looked as if they wouldn't get that far.

"Yeah, Montana," Ray lied. "I just gave her the new demo."

"Don't worry, Ray." Cory smirked. "I'm sure she'll listen to anything *you* give her."

"Okay, okay. But since it isn't my love life we're trying to hire someone for," Ray reminded him, "what are we going to do about the band?"

"You mean which of the long list of unspectacular musicians do we want to play with?" Austin asked. "No one is leaping to mind."

"I agree," Cory said. "We want to be better, not more mediocre."

"So what should we do?" Austin groaned. "Have another audition?"

"Maybe you can audition me?"

They all turned. Ray smiled.

Karin was standing in the doorway, clutching a tape in her right hand. She looked at Ray.

"I played it," she said. "And it's amazing."

"What is *she* doing here!" Austin asked Ray, betrayal showing on his face.

"Look, I'm sorry I didn't say anything about it," Ray explained. "But I heard her at Club Z. You guys didn't tell me how good she is."

"It didn't seem to be the point after the band broke up," Austin said bitterly.

"Listen, when he first suggested it the other night, I said no way," Karin admitted.

"And that's what I say," Austin agreed.

"But then I listened to the music," Karin went on, turning to Austin. "And I thought that it was worth trying. This music is awesome. Exactly the kind of stuff I'd love to be a part of."

"And you guys already know what her voice can do," Ray added.

"Yeah, we know," Cory muttered.

"Maybe this was a mistake," Karin said, crossing her arms.

"Come on, Karin," Cory argued. "You know

I think you have the best voice in the state. But I listened to more fighting than music the last time we tried this."

"I just don't know," Austin said. "We couldn't make it work when we were together, so how could we make it work now?"

"Maybe that was the problem." Karin shrugged. "We were playing together *and* dating. And this time, we'll just be playing together."

Austin looked thoughtful.

"The point is what we're doing this for," Ray reminded them all. "And if it's the music, then there's nothing else to worry about."

"Well, I don't want any of the people we heard this weekend," Cory admitted.

"And we need something," Austin agreed.

"Let's just try a jam," Ray suggested, telling himself not to get too excited. "See how it goes. You heard the songs, right?" he asked Karin. "You think you know the words?"

"Enough," she replied, smiling and walking over to Ray's microphone.

Even before Cory banged out the beat, Ray was feeling good. And when the music started, he felt even better. They'd found the last—and perfect—piece to the Radical Moves puzzle!

# CHAPTER 13

Nancy was standing by her car in the Purity's parking lot, drumming nervously on the roof. Her eyes were glued to the door of the diner. Larry was still inside.

There isn't enough evidence for the police to arrest him, she surmised. But there's enough to be suspicious.

Suddenly she spotted the green sedan she'd seen Larry get out of the other day. It was parked against the far end of the diner.

"I have to stall him," she murmured.

An idea hit her all at once. She knew it was dangerous, but she was pretty sure it would work. She bolted for Larry's car.

Squatting close to the ground, she shuffled toward the front wheel on the driver's side and unscrewed the cap on the air valve.

Please have dessert, she prayed, and extra coffee.

Using the tip of her pen, she leaned hard against the valve. The air hissed out. Slowly, the tire started to collapse.

He'll think it's a flat, she hoped.

The diner door was opening and closing. Nancy heard laughter and low conversation. Footsteps in the gravel parking lot.

Come on! she commanded the tire as it slowly sank.

A couple of minutes later it was flat, and Nancy hurried back to her car. Then she waited.

Okay, he comes out, and he sees he's got a flat and starts to change it, she planned in her head. Then I go over and ask if he needs help. And I start talking to him.

That was as far as Nancy got. The diner door opened again, and there stood Larry, stretching in the sunshine. Nancy watched as he headed toward his car, stopped dead in his tracks, and cursed under his breath. He went around to the back of the car, opened the trunk, and started rummaging around. Then Nancy made her break.

"Got a flat, huh?" she called over.

Larry tossed her a get-lost look over his shoulder. He rummaged some more through the trunk. Nancy heard the sound of clinking metal and other junk. "Can't find the jack," he griped.

"Maybe my jack will fit your car."

"Yeah, what kind of car do you have?"

"Mustang," Nancy replied.

Larry nodded, suddenly polite. "Maybe . . . if you wouldn't mind."

Nancy retrieved the jack from her trunk. But before she brought it over, she had another idea. She got in her car and backed it right behind Larry's, trapping him against the diner. Now he couldn't go anywhere unless she moved.

Nancy passed over the jack. "Thanks," Larry grumbled reluctantly.

"No problem."

As Larry got on his back to set the jack, Nancy casually stepped over to his open trunk. She knew people had a bad habit of filling their trunks with junk. Forgotten junk. Maybe there was something in the trunk . . .

Larry's trunk was full of stuff: rags and a torn blanket, an old gasoline container, a pair of jumper cables, a toolbox, and—

Nancy's eyes stopped on a pair of black leather gloves.

Eileen and George were sprinting the last twenty yards to the Student Union, and George was pulling ahead.

"How can you run like this after a party last night!" Eileen cried, panting heavily as she made one last-ditch effort to keep up. In seconds they were both collapsed on the steps of the building, red-faced and moaning.

"Mostly . . ." George finally managed to answer. "Because you do . . . all the talking . . . when we run."

"Ha, ha." Eileen chuckled. "It's very entertaining for you. So don't complain."

"Good run," George groaned, stretching out her legs. "Boy, I *am* stiff after all the partying this weekend."

"Yeah, I'm glad it's over," Eileen said. "I can't tell you how wonderful it is *not* to hear everybody asking me about Club Z."

"Speaking of Friday night," George teased. "What happened to you guys? I couldn't find you anywhere."

Eileen smiled coyly. "We realized we had another party to attend."

"Oh," George said, catching on. "Real exclusive, I bet."

Eileen grinned. "Only two invitations. Sorry I couldn't get you on the guest list."

"You got me into Club Z, anyway," George said. "So I guess I can let it slide. Besides, now that the club is officially open, we don't need you anymore."

"That's right," Eileen said. "Now that the opening party is over, no more suitemates and friends dropping subtle hints," Eileen continued. "No more sorority sisters dropping obvious threats. I am officially off the hook from any further Club Z social hysteria."

"Good." George chuckled. "Because I'm ready for some lunch hysteria. But I hope this happy-to-be-free-of-Club-Z attitude doesn't mean you won't be joining us all there next weekend."

"By next weekend I'll be happy to talk about Club Z," Eileen replied as she and George jogged up the stairs and made their way to the Student Union snack bar. "As long as I don't have to think about it until Friday night."

Eileen and George had been waiting in the snack bar line only a few minutes when Montana Smith waved to them from a nearby table and hurried over.

"Eileen? I've been looking all over for you," Montana said, following Eileen and George as they pushed their trays along the snack bar. "I have to ask you something really important."

"Shoot," Eileen replied, reaching for a yogurt.

"Do you know who does the booking for Club Z?"

George burst out laughing.

No, Eileen told herself. It can't be happening.

"I have the hottest band in Weston," Montana began. "Ray Johansson's new band, Radical Moves. And Club Z would be the perfect place for them to debut. We're still trying to get Jason on our radio show, and if he books the bands himself, great. But if there's someone else we need to speak to, we figured since you have connections—"

Eileen sighed and closed her eyes as Montana continued to talk. Was it possible that Club Z would be a part of her relationship with Emmet forever? Maybe she should just come out and ask Jason for a job? Because it looked as if she wasn't finished with Club Z yet. Not by a long shot!

"So how did it go?" Bess asked excitedly when Holly finally returned to the Kappa house later that afternoon.

After a few minutes of watching the big meeting between Blondie and Flash in Java Joe's, it had been clear to Bess and George that Flash wasn't an ax murderer or a geek. In fact, he looked adorable and Holly had looked perfectly ecstatic. So Bess had gone over to the Kappa house to study, and George had left for a run. Of course, since then Bess had been waiting eagerly to get the scoop on Holly's new friend. Even George had dropped by the house after her run to hear the gossip.

"Is this the first-date debriefing?" Janie asked, coming into the Kappa living room. "About the controversial computer man?"

"I believe his name was Flash," Soozie mocked.

"Actually"—Holly grinned—"his name is Jean-Marc, and he's an exchange student from Quebec."

"Interesting," Bess said.

"How great for you." Soozie smirked. "I've always wanted to date a guy with a hyphen."

"A *French* hyphen." Janie smiled, turning to

Soozie. "Ahh, the language of romance. Not too geeky, I'd say."

"He's great," Holly went on. "Even better in real life. He's very into the arts."

"And sexy," George added with a nod.

"That's true." Bess chuckled. "We only saw him for a few minutes. But it was a *good* few minutes, if you know what I mean."

"Yes, he's very cute," Holly agreed. "But he's also a wonderful person. We must have talked for three hours."

"So you just sat down and spilled your guts?" Janie asked, shaking her head. "Wasn't it weird?"

"It was awkward at first," Holly admitted. "But he's the same person I've been talking to on the computer. I already know a lot about him, and now I know what he looks like, too."

"Hot," George mouthed, and everyone laughed.

"And," Holly added, "he asked me out for Friday night."

"Way to go!" Janie said.

"I didn't expect this would happen," Holly said. "But I'm not complaining."

"Maybe on-line dating isn't so weird after all," Janie added.

"I'm not even close to being ready for a real date," Bess said quickly. "But it does sound like fun to talk to someone on the computer."

I think I'll have to find out about these chat rooms myself, she mused.

Nancy peeked around the trunk at Larry. "How does the jack fit?" she asked.

Larry grunted. He'd gotten it just behind the flat tire and was beginning to lift the car off the ground.

Satisfied that he was distracted, Nancy leaned in for a closer look. The black gloves she saw were fraying at the fingers. She turned one over. The palm was splotched with stains of some kind. Blood?

The car stopped rising. Nancy heard Larry get to his feet. She leaped back and forced herself to smile up at him.

"Tire iron." He sniffed, and rummaged through his trunk again, burying the gloves. Grabbing the tire iron, he stepped back toward the wheel again, tossing a grudging "Thanks" at Nancy.

"No problem," Nancy replied with forced cheer. Now what? she asked herself. She still needed more evidence. The gloves weren't enough. And maybe it wasn't blood on them. Maybe it was motor oil. Or paint.

Out of the corner of her eye, Nancy picked up a wink of light in the trunk. There, underneath an old car battery Larry had just unearthed, was a gold necklace—but not just any necklace. It fit exactly Jenny's description of the necklace ripped off her neck during her attack!

Nancy swallowed hard. "Hey, you know what, I've got to make a quick phone call over there," she said, pointing at the phone booth. "I'll be back in a sec."

Larry stood to his full, threatening height. "But you blocked me in."

Nancy put on a relaxed, offhanded smile. "I'll be back before you're finished. You still have to dig your spare tire out from under all that junk."

Before Larry could protest, Nancy hurried over to the booth, dropped in some coins, and dialed the police. Two minutes later Larry was standing impatiently beside his car, his hands crossed over his chest, staring at her angrily.

Nancy cast an uneasy glance in his direction. "What do you want me to do?" she asked the officer on the line.

"Stall," the man said. "We have a squad car on the way."

In the distance Nancy could hear the whine of a police siren. She leaned out of the booth and waved at Larry. "I'm tied up on hold!" she called. "I'll be just one minute! Sorry!"

# CHAPTER 14

It was almost four o'clock, and the main conference room of the Alliance Center was jammed with beautiful women and Natural Shades executives. Pam was wandering around, nervously chewing her fingernails. There were Natural Shades banners and placards all over the room and a group of print and television news media people, including a TV cameraman, were loitering in the corner. One entire table by the door was covered in small paper bags with the Natural Shades logo.

"Door prizes for the losers," Reva said, coming up behind Pam. Reva had been with Pam through the first interview with the Natural Shades execs, and she'd also been declared a finalist. Pam noticed that Reva looked as nervous as she felt herself.

"I don't know," Reva said, looking bothered. "I think I may have blown any chance I had."

"What do you mean?" Pam asked. "Natural Shades announced weeks ago that they knew who their new model was."

"I thought so, too," Reva said. She looked around to see who was standing near them, then leaned close to Pam. "But then I turned down Jesse Potter's invitation to spend the night with him."

"You're kidding," Pam said, her mind reeling.

"No, I'm not," Reva answered, embarrassed. "From his reaction," she said, "it was clear I'd make a big mistake."

"You may not believe this," Pam said, "but I think I had the same conversation with him."

Reva's eyes widened. "Did he say something about how 'today is going to be the biggest day of your life'?"

"Exactly," Pam confessed. "He said in just a few days I'd realize how beautiful I really was."

"Which he, of course, noticed right away."

"And how since I'd be working with him there would be lots of opportunities to 'get to know each other better,'" Pam continued, mocking Jesse's voice.

"And how convenient that he just happened to have a motel room where you could begin that long friendship," Reva said.

Pam shook her head in amazement. "I can't believe I was defending him when Jamal was so suspicious. I thought for sure Jesse was just trying to be helpful."

The two women stood looking at each other in silence. "Slime," Reva finally said, her jaw clenched.

"Scum," Pam agreed, shaking her head. "But that's not all."

"What?" Reva asked immediately. "He didn't get physical with you, did he?"

"Not me," Pam said. There was no way she was going to keep this information to herself.

"I was out for a run this morning," Pam began. "Early, because I was nervous about all this." She waved at the excited crowd around them. "I just happened to be up near the College Motel. And who should come outside?"

"No," Reva said breathlessly. Pam could tell from her expression that Reva knew what was coming next.

"Yes," Pam replied. "It was Jesse. And he wasn't alone."

"I don't believe it!" Reva cried. "That's so disgusting. Who would have fallen for that gross line of his?"

"Tamara."

Reva's jaw dropped, but when nothing came out, she slowly closed her mouth.

"Attention, everyone!"

Pam and Reva both turned. Jesse Potter was standing at the front of the room. A trim, handsome woman in a business suit stood next to him.

"A few of you may remember me," Jesse began.

"Only a few?" Pam heard Reva mutter. "Isn't that a shame."

"But I just helped to take all those beautiful photos of you ladies," Jesse went on. "Now I'd like to introduce the woman who's about to change one of your lives. Sharice Jones, president of Natural Shades Cosmetics."

"First I'd like to thank each and every one of you," Ms. Jones began. "You can all pick up your free samples of the new Natural Shades line before you leave. But I know what you're all waiting for, so I won't delay." She reached into her bag and pulled out a slip of paper. "We're all happy and proud to announce the new Midwest model for Natural Shades Cosmetics—"

Pam held her breath.

"Tamara Franklin!"

Squeals of excitement rose from the front of the room. Pam watched as Tamara made her way up to the podium. Amazingly, the first thing she did was throw her arms around Jesse's neck and plant an enormous kiss on his lips.

"Is she trying to advertise what went on?" Reva asked, turning to Pam.

Pam just shrugged, embarrassed that for a few hours she'd really begun to believe that she'd won. She started chuckling at herself. "Okay, I'm disappointed. I just wonder how much, if anything, Jesse really had to do with it?"

Reva shrugged. "If he was the ticket to the winner's circle, I'm not sorry I didn't take it."

Pam nodded. "Do you think we should let the company know what he's doing? He may have done this with women all over the country."

"I don't know," Reva admitted. "But I can't imagine that Natural Shades would be happy to know the way they were being represented."

"You mean by the Natural Jerk," Pam said.

"Exactly," Reva said. "It's funny, you know. Jesse is so awful, but meeting him has actually made me feel really great about myself."

"What do you mean?" Pam asked.

"First of all, that I'm no Tamara Franklin. And second, I may have dreams about my life, but when it comes to boyfriends, my dreams have already been answered."

"So have mine," Pam said, smiling as she thought of Jamal. Then she took Reva by the arm and headed for the front door. "Let's get our booby prizes and cut out of here."

It wasn't until Nancy was crossing the quad toward the *Wilder Times* office that she realized how nervous she was about how Gail would take the news of what she'd done. She definitely didn't want to lose her status at the paper. She thought the best thing to do would be to give Gail what she'd asked for: the Trisha Evanson profile.

But before she could take another step, she felt a small, soft hand grab her around the wrist.

"I've been looking all over for you." It was Trisha Evanson. And she was clutching her books to her chest, crying. "Thank you. You've helped save my brother by finding that other guy."

Nancy smiled at her. "How did you know so quickly?"

"Cal's lawyer called me," Trisha replied excitedly. Her voice turned serious, and her eyes darkened. "It'll be a while before it's made public that Cal is innocent. The police said they don't want any more mistakes. They want to investigate Larry thoroughly."

Nancy nodded. "It's terrible, what you two have gone through in the last few years."

Trisha flashed a brilliant smile. "But Cal's going to be free now! Cal really wants to meet you. Will you?"

Nancy laughed softly. It was all confusing and exciting at the same time.

"I'll meet Cal," she said. "But first I have to write a story. In fact, it's about you."

Trisha blushed. "I don't think *I'm* the real story anymore," she said. She gently pressed a finger against Nancy's arm. "You are."

"I'll call you later," Nancy replied.

As soon as she entered the newspaper office, Gail walked up to her.

"Can I see you in my office?" she asked.

Nancy followed her.

"The DA just called me," Gail said over her

shoulder. "He told me the police have a new suspect. A *real* suspect."

Gail closed the door to her office. Jake was already inside, leaning against the wall. He crossed the floor and wrapped her in a tight hug. "I'm proud of you," he whispered in her ear.

But when he released her, Nancy could feel something had changed. She didn't know what. But it had something to do with the way he touched her. Or maybe it was the way he didn't touch her. Or maybe it was just her.

"So," Gail said, "you still haven't written the story I asked you to."

"I know," Nancy said quickly. "That's why I came over right away. I'm almost done. It'll be ready by deadline."

Gail held up her hand. "I'm taking you off that story, Nancy," she said. "And putting you on the wrap-up and analysis."

"That's *your* piece, Gail," Nancy protested.

"Not anymore. You took it right out of my hands. Both of our hands, actually." Gail threw Jake a resigned look.

Jake shrugged. "Gail's right. You deserve it."

"The fact is, I couldn't be prouder," Gail added. "You believed in your side of the story, and you did just what Steve said to do. You didn't give up. All along I thought I was the one fighting for the right story. But I was wrong."

Nancy was about to tell Gail she knew about her and Joan Rostenkowski, but she stopped herself. What was the point? The case was solved. Joan had fingered Cal for her own reasons and had used Gail to do it. Joan might have been mad at him for something. Maybe Cal had broken up with her, and she wanted revenge.

Nancy figured that Gail probably felt terrible. If she knew Nancy knew, she'd just feel worse.

"So tell us," Jake said excitedly, "what's the scoop? How did you know?"

Nancy took a seat, then told them about Larry's bandaged hand and the tattoo, and then how she tricked him into opening his trunk.

"That," Jake said with a belly laugh, "is brilliant! Remind me never to get on your bad side."

"The police found a judge to sign a search warrant for Larry's apartment on a Sunday," Gail told Nancy. "They found some of the jewelry that Larry took from his victims. Believe it or not, he still had some of it. And the ski mask they all described was also in the apartment.

"Apparently, the reason the earlier victims didn't know about Larry's tattoo was that it was hidden under his gloves. Jenny was the only one who got a look at it. And the preliminary lab report on those gloves confirms that they were stained with human blood."

"What I still don't get is why he came back to Weston," Nancy said, shaking her head. "He'd gotten away with everything. Cal Evanson was in jail."

"He got cocky," Gail said with a shrug. "He

moved to Ohio during the first police investigation. But when the media started splashing the crime all over the news again, and there still wasn't any mention of him—well, he just got arrogant. He said he wanted to come back to Weston and check out the media circus for himself."

Nancy was nodding. "But once back at the scene of the crime, he had to commit another crime," she said. "It's classic." She shook her head mournfully. "I should have guessed."

"How could you?" Jake said sympathetically.

Nancy looked at Gail. "You still did the right thing," she insisted, "by not giving up that name."

"Even if I was dead wrong," Gail replied.

Jake shrugged. "We can't always be right."

Nancy smiled slightly at the irony of Jake's comment. Jake looked up, surprise on his face, as if he'd realized what he'd said, too.

Jake sat next to Nancy and reached for her hand. "I'm really sorry," he said dejectedly.

"Well!" Gail exclaimed, pushing herself out of her chair. "That's my cue. I think I'll leave you two alone for a while." She patted Nancy on the shoulder as she passed. "I'm not happy you didn't follow my orders, but I respect you for sticking to your principles. It's probably what I would have done."

When the door closed behind Gail, Nancy asked, "What about you? How do you feel?"

"I agree with her," he replied.

Nancy furrowed her brow, surprised. "You do? Last night you didn't sound so sure."

"But the real question," Jake said, "is how do *you* feel?"

Nancy studied his face. She didn't know what she was looking at anymore. She still loved him, but she could feel the rift between them growing, even as they sat there holding hands. Something she once loved and needed had slipped away.

She gave his hand a squeeze, then leaned between the chairs and kissed him on the lips. From this close, she could see herself in his beautiful, soft eyes. She let her fingers drift through his hair, touching the sides of his face, touching his lips.

All she wanted to know was if could they get back whatever was gone. She knew she wanted to. "I'm not sure how I feel," she said sorrowfully. "I'm just not sure."

Frustrated, Bess pushed her books away and leaned back against the couch. She was sitting on the floor of the Kappa house living room on Sunday night, trying to focus her mind on both Western civ *and* biology. Unfortunately, she was doing so much studying, she was beginning to mix everything up.

Of course the real reason Bess was having trouble studying was because she couldn't stop thinking about her audition with Jeanne Glasseburg. Ms. Glasseburg had said she'd call, but still, Bess hadn't heard.

She'd given the acting coach the number of her dorm room and the Kappa house, so there was no way Bess could blame a missed message.

Maybe she's not calling me because it's bad news and she doesn't want to hurt my feelings, Bess thought. Maybe she thinks I just flip out all the time.

Bess hadn't completely broken down at her audition, but she knew she'd cried a little. If Ms. Glasseburg thought Bess would also cry in class every day, there was no way she'd invite her into the special seminar.

Just then the house phone started ringing, and Bess leaped up, calling out that she'd answer it.

"Hello?"

"Bess? Oh, hi. This is Jeanne Glasseburg."

"Yes?" Bess asked, her heart pounding so loudly in her chest she was sure that the acting coach could hear it.

"I've made my decision about your audition," Ms. Glasseburg went on. "I'd like to offer you a place in my class next semester."

Bess was so shocked she couldn't reply. And then, in seconds, she was smiling so hard her cheeks hurt.

"Bess? Bess, are you there?"

"Yes," Bess choked out happily. "Thank you. Thank you so much!"

"Don't thank me," Ms. Glasseburg said. "Your

second scene was wonderful. But next semester I'll expect you to get that first one right."

"I will," Bess promised.

"We'll see each other in the spring term then," Ms. Glasseburg said before hanging up.

Carefully, Bess placed the receiver back in its cradle. "I did it," she said, hardly able to believe it.

The moonlight shone through the big bay window as Bess walked back into the living room and sat on the couch. For a few moments, Bess watched her sorority sisters rush in and out. Then her eyes drifted to the window and out over the Wilder campus—the old brick buildings covered with ivy, the street lamps crisscrossing the quad. For the first time in a long while, Bess felt contentment wash through her.

I finally have something to look forward to, Bess thought.

She leaned back and threw her legs over the arm of the couch and settled in to watch the moon cross the sky. She closed her eyes for a moment and remembered the many nights she'd spent watching the stars with Paul—how they would hold each other and talk about their dreams. Bess smiled and opened her eyes.

I'll never stop missing Paul, she said to herself. He'll always be the first real love of my life. But now I'm moving on.

## NEXT IN NANCY DREW ON CAMPUS™:

Soozie Beckerman thought her sorority sister Holly was crazy: surfing the Internet, looking for a date. But who's crazy now? Holly ended up with a gorgeous guy, and Soozie's ended up on-line, searching for her own perfect connection. And she seems to have found him—until Mr. Wonderful's messages start turning very, very weird. Nancy turns computer sleuth, and it may be easier to find a solution to Soozie's problem than her own: uncrossing the wires between her and Jake, *and* her and Terry. Stephanie, meanwhile, doesn't need to go on-line to send out all the wrong signals. Her flirting may have crossed the line, and Jonathan isn't sure he wants her back at all . . . in *Love On-Line,* Nancy Drew on Campus #19.

# Nancy Drew on Campus™

# By Carolyn Keene

- ❏ 1 New Lives, New Loves 52737-1/$3.99
- ❏ 2 On Her Own 52741-X/$3.99
- ❏ 3 Don't Look Back 52744-4/$3.99
- ❏ 4 Tell Me The Truth 52745-2/$3.99
- ❏ 5 Secret Rules 52746-0/$3.99
- ❏ 6 It's Your Move 52748-7/$3.99
- ❏ 7 False Friends 52751-7/$3.99
- ❏ 8 Getting Closer 52754-1/$3.99
- ❏ 9 Broken Promises 52757-6/$3.99
- ❏ 10 Party Weekend 52758-4/$3.99
- ❏ 11 In the Name of Love 52759-2/$3.99
- ❏ 12 Just the Two of Us 52764-9/$3.99
- ❏ 13 Campus Exposures 56802-7/$3.99
- ❏ 14 Hard to Get 56803-5/$3.99
- ❏ 15 Loving and Losing 56804-3/$3.99
- ❏ 16 Going Home 56805-1/$3.99
- ❏ 17 New Beginnings 56806-X/$3.99
- ❏ 18 Keeping Secrets 56807-8/$3.99

Available from Archway Paperbacks